Eric

THE

MURDER

An addictive crime mystery full of twists

ROY LEWIS

JOFFE BOOKS

Revised edition 2019
Joffe Books, London

First published in Great Britain as *Premium on Death*, 1986

ISBN 978-1-78931-265-2

CHAPTER 1

'The bottom line is,' the accountant said, 'you have by way of disposable assets some £3.5 million. Immediate.'

Silence fell in the room. Beyond the library windows Eric Ward could see the slope of the meadows down towards the river, and beyond, the rising hills towards the Cheviot. It was mid-morning and the sun was bright and hard, glinting on the river. A flock of seagulls wheeled above the ploughed fields across the meadow, thirty miles inland, black against the sunlight.

Anne's eyes were upon him. He looked at her expressionlessly. There was a vague shadow in her glance, an indeterminate anxiety. But he could not help her.

He had listened while the accountant had explained things to her.

'Under the terms of your father's will, as I understand it, certain properties and investments were not to fall in under your control until February of this year. You issued instructions regarding the properties, and the investments, we would now advise you, should be looked at again. The net result as far as your estate is concerned is that you have available to you a considerable cash flow, a net asset, a *realizable* asset, of some significance.'

Over three million pounds' worth of significance. Eric's skin felt cool. The young lawyer who worked for Anne, Mark Fenham, was drumming his fingers lightly on the table. Eric was aware the man had had several consultations with the accountants: Anne had asked for a report to be made. This morning was the result. She had asked him to be present in the library when the discussion was started. He was not certain why she had made the specific request.

Or maybe he did know, but was not prepared to admit it to himself.

Anne was handling the manila folder the accountant had given her as though she expected it to contain a bomb. She was nervous, not so much that the other two men in the room would notice, but enough for Eric to realize that she was suffering from a degree of tension, probably induced by his own presence. Or maybe by his silence.

'You've made various proposals in these papers,' she said. The accountant was called Hoskins. He was about thirty years of age and had not lost the enthusiasm of a young man asked to spend other people's money. His bright blue eyes were gleaming as he leaned forward, long freckled fingers interlaced urgently as he spoke. 'Your father . . . his Lordship . . . has already left you in Morcomb Estates a fairly wide range of investments in land, timber and property. I've checked and these investments and they are, of course, long term. Some of the farms are perhaps not satisfactory performers . . .' He paused, cast an uncertain glance in the direction of Mark Fenham, and hurried on. 'I am advised, on the other hand, that certain social obligations would prevent you disposing of those assets . . . So, in general, the portfolio presently held by Morcomb Estates is a sound one and we would recommend only minimal changes, at the fringes, perhaps.'

'But this is all separate from the assets you're now talking about?' Anne asked, avoiding Eric's eye.

'True. The remainder that comes to you under your father's will is the result of overseas investments that were subject to time constraints: these can now be called in *should* be called in — and added to your estate.'

'But not as part of Morcomb Estates?'

'That is, of course, for you to decide, Mrs Ward. *We* would advise, however, that if you are to take maximum advantage of tax arrangements these sums should not be placed under the control of your existing company. The investment spread should be extended and we have made various suggestions . . .'

Anne raised her head as the silence grew around them again.

'What do you think, Eric?'

'I'm a lawyer, not an accountant.'

'But I respect your judgement.' Her eyes said something else: they said *you're also my husband.*

'My judgement on these matters may well be faulty,' he replied. 'Mark, now, he's different. He's a company lawyer. He should be able to give you sound advice on possibilities and tax advantages of the proposals made.'

He had not intended to emphasize the word *should.* He was not certain he had done so: perhaps the emphasis had merely echoed in his mind. But the shadow moved in Anne's eyes: the uncertainty was being replaced by an edge of anger.

'He had positive suggestions to make.'

'I have read them,' Eric admitted.

'And?'

Eric stretched his legs, rose and walked across to the windows. The sun was warm on his face, the gulls had settled now among the furrows, a greedy, squabbling mass of white. 'I've no direct concern with Morcomb Estates and I'm no company lawyer. The briefing paper Mark's written seems admirable.'

'I would still like to have an opinion from you,' Anne said quietly.

When she lowered her voice it presaged anger. Eric turned and looked at her. It was possible the other two men in the room were vaguely aware of the rising tension and he wanted no quarrel in front of them. He had not wanted to attend this meeting but had done so to avoid a quarrel. He would still avoid it. 'I think, before I express an opinion, I'd like to hear Mark talk about it . . . fill in the background to his proposal.'

His glance locked with Anne's. After a brief pause she nodded, accepting the compromise. She turned to Mark. 'Can you sketch out the proposals for us?'

He was only a few years older than Anne, closer to her age than Eric. He was young, confident and good-looking, and she liked him. He was an able lawyer, and since he had joined the board of Morcomb Estates he had certainly made his mark. If there was an undercurrent of ambition that was no bad thing; if there were hints of impatience in the stretching for goals, it could be the way success was often gained. Eric liked him, but with reservations. The trouble was he could not be certain whether the reservations had personal or professional roots.

Fenham smiled at Anne. It was an easy, confident smile, a reflection of their relationship. 'I'd be happy to talk about the proposals, Anne. The first thing I should say, however, is that they're not entirely my idea — Mr Hoskins here was of considerable assistance when I was searching the market and making the contacts.'

Hoskins glowed.

'I should also add that when I came up with the proposal, and was writing it up, I put it to Hoskins and he checked it out. I gather he approved, in financial and tax terms.' Hoskins nodded. He approved.

'So,' Fenham continued, spreading his hands elegantly, 'what does it all boil down to? In a nutshell, this. In the briefing I've given you, together with the supporting financial statements and negotiating stances, I'm suggesting you consider the possibility of making an investment in an acceptance house. In other words, taking shares in Martin and Channing, of Lombard Street.'

'Acceptance house . . .' Anne murmured.

Hoskins cleared his throat. 'For over a hundred years the simplest and most profitable way of raising a loan in the City was by way of the bill of exchange. This commercial paper, a sort of IOU, has been as good as cash once *Accepted* was written across the face of it. It could then be sold, for slightly less than its value at maturity — usually three months ahead — to a specialist bank in the money market.'

'Discount houses,' Mark Fenham added.

'The system worked,' Hoskins continued, 'because the exporter got his money right away, less the discount. And the importer obtained three months' breathing space before the bill matured, and he had to pay whoever owned the bill.'

'And the acceptance house—'

'Traditionally, one of the privileged group of houses which could accept the bills. They could earn a margin of 1.5 or 2 per cent on the value of each bill accepted.'

'Good business,' Eric said quietly, 'but as I understand it, things changed some five years or so ago.'

Hoskins blinked. 'Well, yes, that's so. Bills are still discounted, of course, but the special privileges of the accepting houses were ended by the Bank of England in 1981. There was no special status given to their endorsement — theirs was no longer the *only* "eligible paper" that the Bank of England would buy.'

'On the other hand,' Fenham interrupted, staring at Eric, 'the commercial possibilities of the system meant that a large number of commercial banks got on to the list. They realized it was good business and there were profits to be made.'

'Profits which would tumble, no doubt, as soon as the number of houses on the list became extensive, and competition sharpened the rates that would be made available to the market.'

Fenham's glance hardened and an edge came into his tone. 'There's no doubt that competition has reduced the profits. But do remember, the old system made so much money it founded dynasties. Yes, they groaned and said goodbye to what had been money for old rope in many cases. They lived like fat cats for decades, and how they had to compete. But there's another side to it. There are still considerable profits to be made in the business. It can form the base from which to launch other business. And it's made the surviving companies keener, sharper in the field.'

'And Martin and Channing are one of the sharp ones?'

'They are,' Fenham said snappishly. 'To begin with, they are old-established, and have managed to retain their membership of the Accepting Houses Committee.'

'Oh, come on,' Eric said, 'that group has no standing now.'

'*Not* quite accurate, Mr Ward,' Hoskins bubbled. 'It remains an elitist club, and has perhaps been overtaken by events, but it is still based on the idea that any member that found itself in difficulties would be supported by the others—'

'But the Bank of England would do that.'

'—and its members are closely vetted. I mean, no *foreign* bank is allowed to join and if the Bank of England is ever asked about the status, financially, of any of the members, the answer would be one word: *undoubted*.'

Mark Fenham cleared his throat. 'It's all in the folder I've given you, of course, but the other advantage that Martin and Channing possess is that they can show a diversified range of business. The firm does a considerable amount of business by way of fees received for underwriting or giving financial advice, against a cost to the bank of the salaries of the comparative few who execute the business. The banking side, which includes foreign exchange dealing and the trade in acceptances, remains very important, but they also take sizeable corporate finance fees for arranging mergers and company reconstructions. Assets management is also a profitable sideline by way of business. I've given the published earnings of Martin and Channing in the papers you have before you. There's also an estimated breakdown of the earnings arising from each kind of business.'

'And there is a further advantage of entering this particular field, of course,' Hoskins added eagerly. 'Merchant banks like Martin and Channing offer advantages denied to virtually all other houses. They are allowed to use a provision of the Companies Act that entitles them to transfer undisclosed sums from their profit-and-loss accounts to reserves, and to keep part of those reserves hidden.'

'The net result,' Fenham said drily, 'is that both the earnings and reserves are likely to be understated. In some cases the true figure, both of earnings and reserves, is probably half as much again as the one disclosed.'

Eric raised his eyebrows. 'Doesn't that mean that the figures you've shown in your briefing paper are — or could be — inaccurate?'

'They'll be on the low side,' Fenham replied after a pause.

'How do you know that?' Eric persisted. 'If the system allows for inaccurate declarations regarding profit, loss and reserves, how can we be sure Anne would be buying into a healthy organization?'

'Their words—'

'Come *on*! Based on their *status* as members of the Accepting Houses Committee, a ghostly status irrelevant to modern business, and merely a group of people fooling themselves that their elitist existence has remained untouched by commercial reality!'

'The theory,' Hoskins said hurriedly, attempting to smooth over the edge of hostility arising between the two lawyers, 'is that by manipulating figures behind the scenes the merchant bank can even out its performance between good and bad years—'

'And raise finance from gullible amateurs who are fishing in financial waters too deep for them,' Eric replied. 'How many investments into merchant banking have *you* negotiated, Mr Hoskins?'

The young accountant flushed and blinked. 'I don't see that as a relevant question, Mr Ward. It's true my experience in that direction is limited, but the principles and the theories on which they are based—'

'What about you, Mark?' Eric asked.

Mark Fenham's eyelids drooped. He gave the impression that the turn of conversation was distasteful to him. He glanced briefly and coolly in Anne's direction, and then looked back towards Eric. His tone was controlled, but there was an edge of contemptuous malice in his voice as he replied. 'Like Mr Hoskins, I have never negotiated a deal with a merchant banking and acceptance house. But for that matter, neither have you, I imagine. On the other hand, I am a company lawyer — which, I believe, is a designation you would not extend to yourself since your practice at the Quayside is, by reputation, somewhat general and low key. As a company lawyer I am in contact with various business interests and am involved in the activity, through Morcomb Estates, of various banking houses. Moreover, if you will permit your age and experience to be counterbalanced by my background, it is perhaps relevant to add that my father was a company accountant who rose to head a large investment company in the south and I have been accustomed to living in an environment where business deals of this kind were commonly discussed over the dinner table. I'm not certain that second-hand experience of this kind is all that valuable, but I would question whether you could claim yours — as a police constable in the back streets of Newcastle before you became a solicitor — makes you any better qualified to judge the merits of the proposals I have made to your wife.'

'Mark—' Anne said warningly.

'I'm sorry, Anne,' Mark Fenham interrupted coolly. 'I am employed by Morcomb Estates as its company solicitor, and in that capacity I was called upon to advise whether or not the sums accruing to you now should be ploughed into the company. The easy reply would have been to do so. I felt it incumbent upon me to look at other possibilities. Mr Hoskins and I have looked at these, and we are each convinced that the proposals we make are sound. But it's your decision. What I am concerned about is the feeling that the suggestions I make are unwelcome—'

'I asked for your advice, Mark—'

'And I've given it. Your husband seems to dispute not the advice itself so much as the experience and commitment that backs it. I resent being called a gullible amateur, and I feel it is an insult also to Mr Hoskins's professional status. But I've no more to say on the matter. The briefing is there before you. I shall await your instructions in due course. I think it would be appropriate now for me to withdraw.'

It was a cool, dignified, elegant exit. Mr Hoskins made his exit more hurriedly, and was unable to prevent an unfortunate bobbing of the head as he did so.

The silence they left behind them was hostile.

* * *

'What the hell's got into you, Eric?'

He had been asking himself the same question. His head was beginning to ache and there were dangerous pricklings at the back of his eyes, reminding him that tension could always bring back the reality of his glaucoma. He turned his back to Anne and stared angrily out of the window: the sun was shadowed and above the hills clouds gathered, presaging rain.

'I didn't want to come into this meeting,' he offered

'I invited you because I wanted you to be here. As my husband, and because I respect your advice. But at least I expected you to give unbiased advice!'

'Unbiased?'

'The language you used,' Anne snapped, 'and the attitude you adopted seemed to suggest you had other reasons than doubts about the wisdom of the proposals—'

'What are you talking about?' Eric was angry and disturbed, or he would not have seized upon the suggestion. He was aware of a certain irrationality of mood, a restlessness he could not account for, a feeling that all was not well both emotionally and physically. The words were out before he could restrain himself and his heart sank: they could lead to a discussion he wanted to avoid.

Anne was staring at him with wide eyes. 'What am I talking about? I'm not sure really. Not sure because I can't understand the attitude which I *think* you have.'

'Anne—'

'I'm aware you've always had reservations about our . . . relationship. You've always been stupid enough to think that the discrepancy in our ages is important. It may be to you — it certainly isn't to me! And then, the fact that your background and mine are so different, that's been a worm inside your head, not mine, and it seems to have been made worse by the fact that my father left me a wealthy woman. I *know* all about that. I know you have a sense of pride that makes you feel you have to be your own man. That's all right — and though I don't understand the way you work it out of your system, in that crummy office down at the Quayside, all right, I don't basically object, even if I think you'd do better for yourself — and for *me* — if you were more closely involved in Morcomb Estates.'

'Anne, we've been over all this—'

'No, we haven't! Not to the stage where we each did some really plain talking about it. The fact is, you seem to be soured, in a way I can't understand. I've told you — I understand you want to pursue your own career, but must that be at the expense of helping me when I need you?'

'Anne, I don't want to quarrel about this—'

'But that's what is so *frustrating* about you!' Her voice had risen and she was clenching her fists, tears in her eyes. 'You'll never *argue* with me. You treat me like a child, walk away, protect me from emotional violence. But if you can bottle these things up, I can't, and it's time we had it out. I love you and I want your help, but all you see is a spoiled young woman wanting to give you a handout! That's not the way of it!'

He stared at her, aware of the justice in her argument but unable to accept the consequences of it, held back by the devil of independence that dried words in his throat. He shook his head. 'I'm sorry, Anne—'

'But tell me, what do you really think about the Martin and Channing proposal? You talked of deep financial waters and gullible amateurs but the rest of your comment was of the knocking kind. Nothing positive to say — merely running down the honest suggestions two qualified supporters were making.'

The prickling had grown more noticeable behind his eyes.

Irritated, Eric said, 'If I was wrong in using such phrases as gullible amateurs—'

'You *were* wrong!'

'All right, but let's look at the facts. I've read the portfolio Hoskins and Mark Fenham have presented to you, more closely, perhaps, than I've admitted. Contrary to what you seem to believe, I *do* have your best interests at heart, and there are warning signs for me in those papers. I can't back off from the fact that both Hoskins and Fenham are walking down trails new to them — and that's dangerous where large amounts of money are involved. *Your* money. Secondly, the warning bells get louder for me when I hear the published accounts may be inaccurate — they may make more money than they admit. For me, that means they may make *less* money than they admit, too! The Accepting Houses Committee argument is thin — will your investment be bailing out a house that is high on status but low on financial stability and business opportunity? But maybe the major argument that churns over in my mind is one we didn't even get around to—'

'Maybe because you were so rude that they walked out!'

'The fact is, nowhere in these documents is there a firm proposal about what you get out of the deal — other than status, a return on capital, and the knowledge that your money is locked away in financial wheeling and dealing.'

'What else would I be looking for?' Anne asked wildly.

'Control.'

'You want to take *over* Martin and Channing?'

'Of course not. But if you're being asked to plough in a large percentage of three million pounds what control are you going to be offered over the way in which that money will be used?'

'That would be a matter for negotiation with the partners in the banking house.'

'I know it — but there's nothing in the papers prepared by Mark Fenham that lays down the negotiating position you should be adopting, or a forecast of the stance that the directors of Martin and Channing are likely to adopt. Maybe that's why I was tempted to talk about gullible amateurs!'

'Or maybe it was something else,' Anne said angrily. They were both silent. After a short interval Anne walked unsteadily across the room and helped herself to a glass of sherry from the decanter on the far table. She sipped at it, then turned to face Eric.

'Something else,' she repeated.

He didn't want this discussion. 'Look, let's just leave off at this stage. I'm sorry if I was difficult, but—'

'No, we can't leave it now. Let's have it out. There is something else. It's Mark, isn't it?'

Woodenly Eric replied, 'I don't know what you mean.'

'I've had a feeling . . .' Anne frowned. 'It's not been constant, but there was an occasion once up on the crags, when we were in a shooting party and you were watching us, me and Mark, as we walked back together . . . There have been one or two other occasions . . .'

'You're talking nonsense.'

'Am I? Perhaps. Even so . . . let me ask the question. Do you think Mark and I are having an affair?'

His mouth was suddenly dry. 'Of course not.'

'Or maybe are heading towards one.'

'Anne, really—'

'He's attractive. He's more my age than you are — you've said so. We spend a fair amount of time together, with the company, and he's often enough a guest at this house. Why shouldn't you think we might be heading for a closer relationship?'

Eric stared at her. Anne's face was flushed and her voice slightly unsteady as she goaded him. Maybe she wanted the quarrel he would never give her: he couldn't be sure. 'I've told you — you're talking nonsense.'

'I'm not so sure. I've been aware of a certain tension between you and Mark on occasions and I've not been at all clear why it's arisen. It could be you're jealous of him.'

'I see no point in continuing this conversation—'

'The trouble is,' Anne insisted, 'if you are feeling this way why haven't you raised it with me? It makes me wonder whether if it *was* true you'd simply stand back and let it happen.'

'Anne, really—'

'Well, would you? I seem to recall you didn't exactly fight to keep your first wife, did you?'

Something knotted in Eric's stomach and he stared at Anne. Her breathing quickened; she was aware she had hurt him but the blow had been struck and there was no going back now. Panicked, she blurted out, 'You'll say that was different, but what confidence do I have left? You won't discuss these matters with me, so what am I left to suppose? What is certainly clear to me is that your professional judgement is seriously clouded where Mark Fenham is concerned. He has merely been doing his job, and has offered what seems to me to be sound professional advice, backed by financial support from Hoskins. You dismiss both of these people out of hand, and I'm left with the feeling that you lack balance in your judgement. Whether that's the result of professional or personal jealousy, or both, it's for you to say. I can't see any other reason for your behaviour.'

'The reason is I don't want to see you making a fool of yourself and throwing money away.'

'Dammit, it's my money!'

Eric stared at her silently. Maybe that was precisely the problem.

* * *

On the wall of Eric Ward's office on the Quayside at Newcastle was a photograph taken in the 1880s of shipping clustered on the Tyne. The building that housed his office was discernible, as was the Customs House and the Tyne Bridge itself, erected in the 1840s, but the rest of the scene presented a radical change. The river was alive with masted vessels of all nationalities, barges hauling coal from the staiths to make the journey south to hungry industries, commercial shipping flooding in to take on a wide range of commodities and bring in trade from Germany and Denmark, France and the Netherlands.

The scene from his window was quite different now. The masts had gone, as had much of the shipping. Moorings near the Tyne Bridge now were empty often as not, though there was still a reasonable amount of traffic with northern European countries. And oddly enough, Eric's own practice had begun to increase on the marine side.

When he had taken on his two legal executives he had explained to them that the experience they would get with him would be partly conveyancing and partly criminal: the fatter company and commercial work fell to the larger offices in the city, and he had no intention of competing for matrimonial work with the specialists. Even so, over the few years he had been established there had been a noticeable increase in the sort of work that came into offices located near ports. Had it been of a different kind, commercially, he would have suspected that Anne was using her influence to edge contacts into putting work his way. Morcomb Estates had no interests in shipping, however, and the few contracts he had picked up on Tyneside had now seeded themselves to the Wear and to Cleveland: Sunderland and Middlesbrough shipping companies had been calling for his services. It was still on a relatively minor scale, as was the financial work he undertook on a specialized basis, but it was growing. It had meant that Eric had to take on another legal executive.

The person he had finally selected was a bright young man called Edward Elias. His Tyneside accent was broad, and he hailed from Byker, but he was keen, intelligent and dressed carefully in grey pinstripe and white shirt. He claimed some experience in a marine practice and Eric had tested him.

'What's a maritime lien, Mr Elias?'

'It's the right you have to have a ship, or its cargo, impounded for sale, so you can apply the proceeds of sale to pay off debts against it.'

'Can you give me an example?'

'Bottomry bond.'

'Which is?'

'When the shipmaster borrows money on the ship or its cargo — or both — the document he signs, promising to repay the money, is called a bottomry bond.'

Eric smiled. 'And barratry?'

'That comes up in marine insurance policies. Normally, a ship has to carry out its voyage without delay or the policy is void. But the policy will still be in force if the delay is the result of barratry — you know, any wrongful act wilfully committed by the master, or crew, to the prejudice of the owner or charterer. Sir.'

Eric smiled again. Young Elias would do.

And he had proved to be a good acquisition. Routine matters coming in from marine insurers could be dealt with directly by him, and the speed and efficiency with which he had dealt with them meant that more business was beginning to flow in. He it was who had probably brought them the Craig Lynch Marine Insurance business. And the *Gloria.*

Eric could see the vessel now, from his office window overlooking the river. A squat vessel flying a Danish flag, she had brought in a cargo of timber and had unloaded a week previously but had remained tied up at the wharfside while a legal wrangle had started. There was some dispute over the ownership of the cargo, but equally an argument was flaring over the vessel itself. Liens had been taken upon her by a French insurance company but had been discharged on the unloading of the cargo. The files lay on Eric's desk, with copies of judgements from a French court and a Crown Court hearing against the master. People were apparently getting very excited, and there was the danger of the master taking matters into his own hands and quietly slipping out to sea, out of the jurisdiction. Craig Lynch Marine had already spoken to Eric several times on behalf of their clients. They still had to issue final instructions. He was expecting them that morning.

While he waited for the phone call, realizing that prompt action would be demanded, he had leisure to think back over the meeting at Sedleigh Hall and his argument with Anne. He knew there was a great deal of justice in her attitude: it was very frustrating for a woman to have a husband who refused to quarrel with her. Equally, maybe she was right in saying he treated her with an indulgently avuncular air on occasions: it wasn't the way he felt about her, but at the same time he was older than she, and could distance himself from time to time from her stances. There had been no accident in the words used by Mark Fenham: *age and experience*. He'd used them deliberately and seriously; maybe it was why Anne herself had seized upon the issue later, in the quarrel that she had tried to promote.

Mark Fenham.

Eric remembered the shooting party on the moors which Anne had referred to. He had been acutely aware of the fine pair she and Mark Fenham made, but he had not since regarded it as a canker in his mind, as Anne seemed to be suggesting. At the same time, he had to admit the possibility of there being some truth in the allegation. Maybe his judgement *was* being clouded by an unadmitted, simmering doubt he held. He had resisted marriage with Anne for two reasons: the one related to the fact that he felt their discrepancy in ages could prove difficult. The second had been the feeling that he needed to retain his independence, make his own way, fight his private battle against the illness that constantly threatened him. He knew there were elements of stubbornness in him that made things difficult for her. But he still wanted the best for her — even if he did not wish to be too closely involved in her business life.

It could smother him and destroy them both.

Even so, he wanted to help. It was the reason why he had made inquiries about the firm of Martin and Channing.

Mark Fenham had been quite correct. The firm was respectable and old-established. It had been founded in Frankfurt in 1880 by an English businessman called Martin, keen to develop foreign exchange business. At the turn of the century Martin had moved his headquarters to London and in 1920 had been accepted into the fold of the Accepting Houses Committee. He had dominated the firm, clearly, until his death in 1930. After that, from what Eric could gather, the firm had been bought up by an investment company that specialized in buying companies needing finance, and new directors had been put in. Thereafter, under the guidance of a director called Leonard Channing it had prospered, according to its literature, and eventually emerged as Martin and Channing.

There had been no noisy acquisitions, and no doubtful business. But it had acquired two subsidiary companies. One was in Yorkshire; the second was located in Newcastle.

Eric couldn't recall ever having heard of the firm so he had looked them up in the northern directories. And one of the names was known to him.

Reuben Podmore.

It must have been twelve or fifteen years ago, now. A Saturday night, in Pink Lane, just above the railway station in Newcastle. Eric Ward had been in the police force then, returning in plain clothes by train from a course at Dishforth. He had left the train at Newcastle and walked up through Pink Lane, heading for the bus station.

The little man was doubled up against the wall, gasping for breath, hands folded across his stomach. The youth who gripped him by the collar was tall and curly-haired; the one with the knife was dark, swarthy-skinned and the more dangerous of the two. They had whirled on Eric as he had advanced up Pink Lane.

The tall boy had looked scared: mugging a defenceless little man in a pinstriped suit was one thing, but he did not care for the purposeful way in which Eric Ward had kept walking up to them. Eric ignored him; he headed directly for the lad with the knife. There was a mouthful of obscenities before the dark youngster lunged at Eric with the knife. The blade ripped through his sleeve and then Eric's fist thudded into the boy's throat. He gave a strangled gasp and dropped the knife; the other boy released their victim and ran. It had all been over in a matter of seconds.

The little man they had been mugging was in a distressed state. Eric attended to him, loosening his collar. The boy with the knife slipped away; not that it mattered a great deal, for Eric recognized him in court three weeks later when he was hauled up on a charge of burglary. The little man in the pinstripe however was turning colour, and after a few minutes stopped breathing altogether.

It was Eric's giving him the kiss of life and his early transmission to hospital that saved his life. Reuben Podmore had never forgotten that.

The odd thing was that over the years they had never met again. Podmore had wished to show his gratitude financially after his release from hospital but Eric had refused; the result had been a regular donation to a charity each year from Reuben Podmore. The charity had always sent an acknowledgement to Eric Ward's address. It had been Reuben Podmore's way of saying thank you. Eric had never made any inquiries as to what his job had been and made no attempt to meet him.

But the name had leapt out of the page at him, when he had looked up the Martin and Channing northern subsidiary, Stanley Investments.

Investment Manager: Reuben Podmore.

Eric was still wondering what to do about it when the telephone rang. It was Craig Lynch Marine Insurance. They wanted Eric to act immediately: the issues had been resolved.

The bottomry bond on the *Gloria* had been dishonoured and the insurers wanted immediate attachment.

* * *

The Quayside was quiet. A few gulls called in desultory fashion, wheeling aimlessly above his head, and there was a steady stream of traffic across the Tyne Bridge, but apart from a few cars parked among the bollards there was little moving along the riverside. The *Gloria* was moored near the old Custom House, her rusted paintwork acknowledging the sorry position she found herself in, warped ironwork on the deck peeling in the sunlight. Eric called to the wheelhouse but there was no reply. He walked along the quay, the length of the ship, but there was no sign of life and the gangplank was unattended.

Eric climbed aboard. There was no one in the wheelhouse, and the hatches were battened down. The quarters were padlocked, as though the master and crew had left the ship to the tides while they went ashore, careless. Eric hesitated, looked around him, not certain what to do. He had expected a conversation with the skipper, maybe an angry altercation. It seemed as though they didn't care. In a sense, it made his task easier.

In the old days, execution of the bond upon a ship, to ensure the maritime lien was enforced, had been a matter of nailing the relevant notice to the mast where it served as a public notice to all and sundry that the vessel was impounded and could not be moved without permission, of the bondholders. Times had changed. Eric was now armed with a roll of Sellotape. He unfolded the notice from his briefcase, and in a matter of minutes had taped it securely to the mast. The gulls wheeled incuriously above him, planing into the breeze.

It was a task easily completed. Craig Lynch Marine Insurance were now protected unless the master was foolish enough to try to sneak the *Gloria* out to sea and beyond the jurisdiction. It was unlikely. Even so, Eric was surprised to find the ship deserted: at the very least a hand should have been left in charge.

He stepped down again to the quay, and strolled along in the sunshine. He checked his watch; it was nearing lunch-time. He thought about Anne, and Mark Fenham's plans, and at last he decided to do what he guessed he had always intended to do, ever since he had recognized Reuben Podmore's name as investment manager for Stanley Investments.

He made his way up Dog Leap Stairs, climbed up Gray Street and turned into the narrow entry that led to the Old Market. It wasn't easy finding the offices of Stanley Investments. A second-floor office above a winding, narrow stair. It was not the best advertisement for a parent company seeking an investment of over two million pounds.

* * *

There was no one in the outer office. It was clearly inhabited by a receptionist/secretary at normal times, but probably she had gone to take her lunch break. The door with the frosted glass window behind the desk was marked with the legend INVESTMENT MANAGER but there was no name appended: clearly, Stanley Investments demanded degrees of anonymity.

Eric could hear voices behind the door so he waited. He looked around him. The premises were small and mean but he saw some small investment in new technology had been made: a microcomputer with a visual display unit stood on a table next to the secretary's desk. Eric could not be sure whether it would be functional, or merely a confidence booster for prospective clients.

Eric waited. Several minutes passed and he began to feel doubtful about the wisdom of his presence at the office. He should perhaps have rung for an appointment, but there would have been a problem in that he had no real business he wanted to discuss with Podmore. He wanted information but a. business appointment would have demanded precise questions. He would necessarily be imprecise: the questions he had were vague.

He had just about made up his mind to forget the whole thing when the voices were raised, came nearer, and the door opened. Two men came out, glanced at him and hesitated. The man behind them was Reuben Podmore.

In the street, Eric would not have recognized him.

It had been a long time, of course, and their acquaintance had been brief The image Eric had retained was perhaps fifteen years old, and time had thickened Mr Podmore silvered the sparse hair on his head and added heavy jowls to the jaw. The eyes had retained the sharp brightness and the pale blue colour Eric recalled, but they were now heavily pouched and stained with disappointment. There were elements of discontent about the mouth as well and Eric gained the impression that the years had not brought Reuben Podmore the happiness and success he had hoped for.

He was saying something to the two men but broke off at the sight of Eric. There was a brief moment of hesitation, a shadow passing over his features and then he smiled vaguely, breaking into his conversation with his companions. 'I'm sorry, can I help you . . . my secretary . . .'

'Please, I called without an appointment,' Eric said quickly. 'And you're clearly busy. My name's Eric Ward. I . . . I was just renewing an old acquaintance.'

Reuben Podmore stared at him, the breath hissing in his mouth. The pale blue eyes widened, and his mouth formed an O which was suddenly converted into a smile. 'Dear me,' he said slowly, and then, more quickly, 'Dear me, dear me, dear me!'

He glanced hesitantly aside to his two companions as though uncertain whether to introduce them, but then thrust his pudgy fist out in Eric's direction suddenly, grabbed Eric's hand and began to pump it, enclosing it in both his warm, damp hands. 'It's been such a long time, my dear boy. You've changed, of course, as no doubt I have. And if I failed to recognize you for a moment there . . .'

One of the two men at his back coughed lightly, and Podmore started guiltily. He looked around, releasing Eric's hand and fluttered vaguely. 'Please, excuse me, an old friend . . . Mr Ward, can I introduce you? This is Mr Daniels . . . from Chicago, I believe?'

'Boston,' Daniels said coldly. 'Way back.'

'I'm sorry,' Podmore murmured, but Eric was left with the impression that Podmore's slip had been deliberate. A slight smile played about the investment manager's mouth, and as he introduced his second companion Eric knew the guess was right.

'And this is Mr Brinkman.'

'Berckman,' the dark, swarthy man corrected him. He slipped a quick, sharp glance in Eric's direction and Eric knew that this man was nobody's fool: he also recognized Podmore's deliberate mistakes, and probably knew the reasons for them. 'Now you've met an old friend, Mr Podmore, we'll keep you no longer,' he said.

Podmore uttered meaningless platitudes, saw them to the stairs and then returned, beaming, to Eric. 'I never could take to Americans.'

'Business colleagues?'

'In a way. A flying visit to Tyneside, with a request for money.'

'From Stanley Investments?'

'Something like that.' Podmore frowned vaguely, as though irritated by the conversation. 'Let's say the business was put my way without my wanting it, I never really liked it, and now it's gone sour I wish to God we'd never had anything to do with it!' He dismissed the frown and smiled broadly. 'But let's forget all that. Believe me, it's so good to see you!'

* * *

The restaurant was almost full but Mr Podmore was well known there, obviously: he and Eric were ushered to a table in the corner, discreetly placed for the management of business. They were mainly businessmen in the dimly lit room: the extensive Italian menu allowed for extended lunch breaks, when the excuse for good eating and drinking would be the business supposedly undertaken.

'Well, well, well,' Reuben Podmore said, 'after all these years!'

He appeared to have brightened; his skin seemed less sallow, the pouches under his eyes less discontented. He had introduced Eric to his two business colleagues at the office, though Eric could not now recall their names, but they had clearly been only too pleased to go their own way, leaving Podmore free to entertain Eric to lunch.

'I had heard you had left the police force,' Podmore said after they ordered, 'and that you had established yourself in the legal profession, but beyond that . . .'

'We never did really keep in touch, although I always received notification of your donations.'

'The gift of life,' Podmore said, smiling wistfully, 'the payment is small enough. Of course, what one does with that life . . .'

'Business is good?' Eric asked.

'It moves,' Podmore replied noncommittally. He waited as the wine waiter poured a little of the Frascati for him to try. He nodded, then after Eric had refused a glass, he raised his eyebrows questioningly.

'I drink but sparingly,' Eric explained, 'and never at lunch. I had an operation for glaucoma a little while back. Alcohol . . . doesn't help.'

They talked for a while, about Eric's illness and about Reuben Podmore's operation for gallstones. The elderly investment manager explained that otherwise he had been healthy enough: the heart attack he had suffered on the occasion of the mugging in Pink Lane all those years ago had never been repeated. 'Careful living helps, of course,' he added, eyeing the glass of Frascati and the plate of *spaghetti carbonara* in front of him. 'However, I don't quite understand how you came to seek me out if it wasn't on a matter of business. Why now, after all these years?'

Eric smiled. 'I have to admit, it's really a matter of chance . . . and there is an element of business.'

'An element?'

Carefully Eric said, 'I have a . . . client, who is interested in merchant banking. It's not a field I have much experience of, and if I'm to give advice . . .'

'Interested in merchant banking,' Reuben Podmore considered. 'That covers a large number of sins. By *interest* you mean *investment*?'

'It's . . . possible.'

Podmore teased the spaghetti with his fork and nodded. 'But how did you connect me with such activity?'

Eric shrugged. 'I looked in the directory. I saw the name Stanley Investments. Your own name sort of leapt out at me.'

'I see.' Podmore was silent for a while. He took a little spaghetti, sipped at his Frascati and considered the matter. Eric gained the impression that Podmore was looking at his past, weighing up the way life had treated him, counting the lost opportunities, and he was aware again of the lines of disillusion around the man's mouth. Podmore sighed. 'Well, how can I assist you?'

Eric hesitated. 'I suppose it's just generalities I'm interested in at this stage. Stanley Investments, for instance—'

'You'll have been surprised at the size and decor of the office, I suppose,' Podmore said briskly. 'It's an interesting fact in the business, you know: the investment banker has a great advantage over other businesses. His presence can be established on quite a modest scale, merely by opening an office and equipping it with telephones and data screens.'

There was an element of defensiveness in Podmore's tone.

Eric frowned. 'So how do you deal with clients who wish to visit you, and who might be put off by a low-level front office operation?'

'Ah, investment banking doesn't work like that. It's true the main office may well be of an impressive kind, in London, but subsidiaries are another matter. Business is actually raised on the basis of confidence — and that's achieved through the tombstones.'

'The what?'

Podmore gave him a faded smile. 'Banks show themselves to the world by buying newspaper space — the *Financial Times*, the *Wall Street Journal.* Sometimes it's just direct advertising; other times it's to do with a specific piece of business, such as one that details the issue of shares or bonds. You can always recognize them — they're commemorative, in that they include a statement like: *All these securities having been sold, this announcement appears as a matter of record only.*'

'Hence the "tombstone"?'

'Correct.' Podmore nodded gravely. 'The trick is, to get your name on the tombstone.'

'I don't understand.'

'The tombstone tells the world the bank has done a great piece of business. But it contains more than one name: there's usually a long list of banks involved. Indeed, an important tombstone will list maybe a hundred: banks don't like it if they're not mentioned in the list. It gives their chairman a warm feeling, to open the newspaper and see the bank listed. It shows the world they're in business.'

'They'll have actually taken part, though.'

'Oh yes, they'll have underwritten a few shares, at least. I mean, the lead manager name appears at the top left; but the firms at the bottom, they're often there just as a gesture. The important thing is they want to be there. It airs the bank's name in a number of countries. It gives them visibility. It allows them to bid and it brings them status. Financial status.'

'Even though the extent of the underwriting is small?'

'Even so.' Podmore grinned. 'If your name doesn't appear on the tombstone, paradoxically, you're really dead!'

'It seems an odd way to go about things,' Eric commented. 'The system must be based on confidence and trust, yet it relies also upon what seems to me to be a confidence trick as far as tombstoning is concerned.'

Podmore poured himself a little more of the Frascati. 'Ah, that's one way of looking at it. On the other hand, markets believe that higher ethical standards apply in the merchant banking world than elsewhere. To that extent Wall Street and the City of London are in the same Anglo-Saxon boat. It's us against the Latins. London still regards itself as superior, of course. It rests on the rather self-indulgent assumption that where Americans are naturally greedy and take the short view, Europeans are thoughtful and see themselves in the context of history.'

Eric laughed. 'Is that how you see it?'

'My parent firm has been in business since 1880. It, and I too, take a long-term view. There have been good times; there can be bad times. If one faces leaner expectations, so be it. Wall Street . . . it tends to be more . . . excitable about the lean times.'

Carefully Eric said, 'Does that mean that business isn't too good at the moment?'

Podmore did not look up from his spaghetti, but there was a space of several seconds before he replied. The casual way in which he pushed his plate aside did not fool Eric: there was an edge of wariness in the man as he said, 'I hope I've not given you that impression. I was merely generalizing.'

'Even so,' Eric persisted, 'competition must have caused problems.'

'Competition has certainly narrowed the banker's turn.'

'The what?'

'The *banker's turn*: the margin between the rate he pays and the rate he receives for money. I mean, it's easy when you get deposits from a trading corporation — you can lend such funds out again at a profitable rate to finance a building project, or a cargo. The margins get considerably narrower on the other hand where the lending and borrowing is wholesale — you know, where you create the deposit by borrowing it more expensively in the interbank market, hoping you'll find someone who'll pay a higher rate.'

'Lending long, and borrowing short.'

'Or vice versa,' Podmore agreed. 'It depends on your estimates of how the rates are likely to move. You can make a lot of money — but the margins are small. And with small margins you've got to deal in large amounts if you're to generate worthwhile earnings.'

'Is that the kind of business you're in at Stanley Investments?' Eric asked.

Again there was a short pause as Podmore eyed his glass. 'No, not really. It's regarded as a little . . . rich for our blood.'

'By whom?'

'You see,' Podmore went on, almost speaking to himself, 'it all depends on almost hourly operations. The executive in charge of such operations in the money market must never be unaware of the limits beyond which his dealers may not go. He is, after all, securing the deposit base of the bank, making sure there's money to lend out at wholesale rates, then checking to ensure it's not lent imprudently.'

Eric sensed something unspoken and his skin prickled. 'That's not the kind of business you undertake?'

'We do a fair amount of underwriting,' Reuben Podmore said sharply, as though he wished to bring the drift of conversation to an end.

'But if you appear on the tombstones—'

'Ah . . . the main course. What is it you ordered? *Pollo al cacciatora* was it not? Can I not tempt you to a little of the Frascati to wash it down?'

* * *

He left Reuben Podmore at the entrance to Stanley Investments at three o'clock. Eric strolled down to the Quayside in the thin afternoon sunshine. The *Gloria* was still moored there, with no signs of life aboard. The water looked black, a thin veil of scum and oil on the surface, and across to his right the Swing Bridge was opening to allow passage of a tanker, manoeuvring its way downstream from the power station beyond Lemington Gut.

He felt vaguely dissatisfied with what he had learned from Reuben Podmore. The conversation about Stanley Investments had come to an abrupt end once Eric's questions became direct; Podmore had been polite, but firm, steering topics away from merchant banking and into less personal waters. He had been a friendly host, and he clearly still retained elements of gratitude for what Eric had done for him years previously. Even so, there was a limit beyond which his assistance would not be extended, and he was wary about discussing the business in which he was involved.

One thing Podmore had let slip inadvertently. While Stanley Investments was the northern offshoot of Martin and Channing, there were no directors located in Newcastle:

Podmore was employed as its investment manager, but he himself held no shares in the firm and took no part in policy-making. Moreover, the business undertaken was of a limited kind. That much Eric had been able to glean from the conversation: the rest was guesswork.

In the first instance, Podmore's explanation — before one was asked for — regarding his office had been too swift and too glib. What he had said had the ring of truth, as a generality, but it did not entirely explain the dinginess of the premises or the lack of staff present there. He had also turned the issue aside when Eric had asked him directly how good business was: Eric had gained the impression Podmore was dissatisfied with the kind of answer he might have been forced to make.

And perhaps Podmore's own air of despondency and disillusionment was a further contributory factor to Eric's view of the situation: it fitted in with the impression that the Stanley Investments subsidiary did not have the confidence of its parent company, Martin and Channing.

The question that now bothered Eric was whether the parent firm itself was high on its credit rating but low on its operational possibilities.

Eric had not discussed the matter further with Anne.

After the outburst and the quarrel they had deliberately avoided the subject of the investment. He was aware that she had told Mark Fenham to go ahead with his presentation, and make contact with Martin and Channing with a view to reaching a draft agreement, but the details had not been discussed with him.

He found himself in some difficulty. Anne had suggested his reticence was ill-founded, and as much concerned with a personal dislike of Mark Fenham as with the business itself. He himself was forced to admit it might be playing a part. On the other hand he had reservations about a possible deal with Martin and Channing, and these reservations had been strengthened by his suspicions after the conversation with Reuben Podmore.

He did not know what to do next.

It was a feeling that annoyed him. He made his way back to the office, dealt with some routine inquiries from each of the legal executives, and after he had given a briefing to young Elias he settled down to some work himself on two draft contracts and a conveyancing matter. The brief needed to go to counsel inside two days and there was the likelihood of a hearing to be fixed in London in a couple of weeks, so it would be an agency matter. It was not something he could leave to the legal executives, so he worked at it himself and the afternoon slipped away.

Before she left, the receptionist called in and made him a cup of tea. Alone in the office, he found thoughts of Reuben Podmore and Martin and Channing intruding upon his concentration. He took a break and sipped his tea, standing at the window, looking out past the *Gloria* to the Gateshead bank and the old ruined church on the skyline.

Pride suggested he leave the issues alone: if she trusted Mark Fenham, and the young lawyer was about to make a fool of himself, that was their problem. But was it pride, or pettiness — and was he really jealous of young Fenham, for his confidence, his easy charm, his smoothness, and the friendliness of his relationship with Anne?

One thing still rankled. She had been wrong to bring up the topic of his first wife, suggesting he had not fought to keep her. That day he had come home and found her with her lover had been traumatic: he had not *wanted* to keep her. It was all long ago now and anything they had had between them was ill-remembered. His relationship with Anne was different, but when did it become necessary to fight?

Perhaps *before* problems arose. Perhaps he should work harder at his marriage, before they drifted apart. And that might mean taking a more positive role in Morcomb Estates and her business life, rather than indulging himself in a back-street business near the Quayside.

Irritated, he turned away, set down his cup and cleared his desk to deal with the conveyancing brief. Eventually Podmore and Morcomb Estates and Martin and Channing receded from his thoughts and he was able to concentrate on the issues before him. It was seven o'clock before he had finished.

It was a long drive back to Sedleigh Hall. He rang Anne, told her there were still a few things he had to do to clear up, and he'd snatch a meal in town before staying at the flat overnight. He expected to be back reasonably early the following afternoon. She was cool, but said she'd be home to greet him. She wouldn't be in Newcastle for a few days: farm auctions in Northumberland, involving Morcomb Estates, would take her to Alnwick.

'By the way,' she added, 'Mark has been in touch with Martin and Channing. You'd better book the date in your diary. We'll be entertaining the senior partner here at Sedleigh Hall in a couple of weeks. There's a chance we'll be finalizing things then. He's called Leonard Channing.'

It soured Eric's appetite. He left his office at eight and walked up the hill to get a snack in the Duke and Duchess. His mood was gloomy: he felt Anne was making a mistake, and he was in no position to offer advice. Its basis would be regarded as jealousy. He felt himself cornered, and annoyed.

He left the pub and walked back down the hill to collect his car and drive to the flat in Gosforth. He got in, drove to the roundabout at Sandhill and glanced back along the Quayside.

He caught a flash of light from the deck of the *Gloria*.

* * *

In a sense it was none of his business. He was a lawyer, not a policeman: those days were long behind him. His connection with the *Gloria* was only through his clients, Craig Lynch Marine, and he had fulfilled his obligations towards them by taping the statutory notice to the mast of the vessel.

But he was curious. He had been aboard and everything had been locked, no sign of master or crew. The notice was affixed, but it was not unknown for a skipper to ignore the notice, slip out of the moorings and vanish out at sea in an attempt to avoid the jurisdiction. It caused problems for Craig Lynch, not Eric Ward: it might in the long run even bring him more business, he thought ruefully.

But if the skipper *was* aboard, and was trying to slip out of the Tyne, and Eric Ward had seen him, his sense of responsibility to his clients demanded he do something about it.

He parked his car near the old Moot Hall and walked back under the roar of the Tyne Bridge until he could see the deck of the *Gloria*.

There was no light on deck, no glimmer from the wheelhouse. Slowly he walked forward, until the hull loomed up above him. He glanced around: no one else seemed to be on the Quayside, although there were some twenty or so cars parked nearby, users of the restaurants that had sprung up near the Side.

On the Gateshead bank the floating restaurant glittered, the coloured festoon of lights coruscating in the dark water, and the rhythmic beat of disco music thudded across to Sandgate. Near the *Gloria*, however, all was quiet. The gangplank was still secure and Eric stepped over the rope, grasped the chain and began to climb aboard.

Downriver a siren mourned and across the Tyne Bridge a police car sped with blue light flashing.

'Anyone aboard?' Eric called.

The light groaning and scrape of the hull against the side of the quay was the only sound he heard in reply. He put out a hand: the rail was greasy. He stepped forward, feeling the sway of the deck under his feet: the tide was on the turn and a light breeze was rising, sweeping in from the coast as the night grew darker. There was a freshness in the air, a hint of rain, perhaps, and he called again, moving towards the wheelhouse.

He could not be certain where he had seen the light. Now, he began to question his own senses: perhaps it had not been a light on the deck, but rather the sweep of a headlight from the Tyne Bridge or the Quayside, a car headlight lancing its beam across the deck, reflecting against the harbour wall. He paused, hesitantly, and looked around him. There was no movement from the Quayside and no sound aboard the *Gloria* except that caused by the lapping tide.

He walked forward to the wheelhouse.

The door was open.

It moved slightly, with the sway of the deck. Inside, everything was dark, and he could make out only vague shapes, unfamiliar to his untrained eye. He put out a hand and held the door, standing there uncertain of how to proceed. He glanced back towards the mast. The pale blur of the taped notice told him it had not been ripped away.

He stepped into the wheelhouse.

Everything happened in a blur. He could not be certain what warned him. It might have been a sound, a movement in the dark, or it might have been the instinctive response bred from his police training. Even as he stepped into the darkness of the wheelhouse he knew suddenly he was not alone, and with the knowledge he was stepping away, thrusting into the cabin and away from the door.

The first blow caught him across the shoulder and he staggered. There was a whirl of movement, the peculiar sensation of warmth as someone closed with him, a hot, fearful body, and then the second wild, swinging blow came.

It caught him across the base of his neck and he gasped, falling forward as his senses swam and a rigid numbness incapacitated him. He fell to his knees, head down, and a nausea came to his throat as the numbness spread along his neck and arm. Behind him there was a rushing, shuffling sound, someone leaping for the doorway and next moment the door was slammed violently and he heard footsteps careering across the deck.

He stayed where he was, unable to speak, head down and gasping for breath as the dreadful numbness held his neck and arm in its grip. He closed his eyes, squeezed them tightly and tried to control his anguished breathing: the nerve ends behind his eyes began to scratch and he tried to calm himself, will away the first tensions that would lead to pain. He kept his head down, waiting, and gradually his breathing slowed, and the numbness in his shoulder was succeeded by a warmth that turned to a painful throbbing.

In a little while that too eased and he climbed to his feet, holding the bulkhead for support. He turned to the door, opened it and stepped out on to the deck.

The breeze was cool to his cheek. He made his way across the deck, vaguely aware that the statutory notice on the mast was still there, and cursing himself for a fool. If the master of the *Gloria* had intended stealing away from the Tyne he would not have done it at turn of the tide, and he would not have been lurking about in the wheelhouse. He would have been down in the engine room if anywhere, preparing to sail.

Eric Ward had no one to blame but himself. An abandoned vessel like the *Gloria* on the Quayside was an open invitation to half the yobbos along Scotswood. The word would quickly be out among the scavengers that the ship was unattended. Once darkness had fallen, someone would certainly be down to find out what was worth stealing. Crews quarters had been locked, but it would not have been difficult to break into the wheelhouse. Eric could not even recall now, from his visit earlier in the day whether the wheelhouse had in fact even been locked.

Moreover, the affixed notice itself may well have been an invitation to the scavengers. But worst of all, he thought disgustedly, It was all none of his business. He had poked his nose m where it was not his concern; he'd disturbed some young thug rifling the wheelhouse where there'd be little of value anyway, and if he now got a sore shoulder and neck as a result it was largely his own fault. He should have minded his own business.

It was likely to have been something heavy, like a piece of iron, to have numbed his neck and shoulder muscles the way it did. He tried to stretch his arm now, as he stood on the deck, and a fierce pain stabbed along his neck and biceps. He headed for the gangway, to make his way back to the Quayside.

Thirty yards away someone was parking a car. Eric made his way down the gangway, stepping over the guardrope and he caught his foot, almost falling. He was still unbalanced, a little dizzy from the two blows he had received. The man near the car was staring at him. A moment later he began to walk forward.

Eric shook his head to try to clear it, and began to walk back towards Sandhill. His step was slow and careful. He heard the man behind him quicken his pace.

'You all right?'

Eric stopped, and nodded. He did not look at the man. He felt vaguely embarrassed at the condition he was in 'I'm all right,' he muttered.

'You look dazed. I saw you come off the boat. I thought you were going to fall.'

'No. Just a bit dizzy. I'll be all right in a moment.'

Eric began to walk away. The man started to walk with him, slowed, and stopped. 'If you're sure you're okay . . .'

'I'll be fine. My car's just along here.'

Eric took a deep breath, cursing. He reached Sandhill and walked slowly towards the old Moot Hall where his car was parked. He had the feeling that the man who had spoken to him was standing in the shadow of the Tyne Bridge, still somewhat solicitous. Two busybodies in one night, Eric thought bitterly. He unlocked the car and got in. He sat there for several minutes before the numbness had eased and the dizziness had gone.

When he finally drove away from the Quayside, swinging around to head for Gray Street and the road out to Gosforth, he saw no lights on the deck of the silent *Gloria*.

* * *

When he woke next morning his arm and neck were stiff and painful; as he waited for the coffee to percolate he exercised his arm grimly, annoyed with himself for boarding the *Gloria* and even more annoyed that he had been caught by the unseen assailant.

During the course of the day the stiffness remained but he was able to work without too much trouble, and he left the office about four to make the drive out to Sedleigh Hall.

He had no great desire to talk to Anne about his foolishness and about the encounter with the thief on board the *Gloria* but he would have been forced into it as soon as she observed how stiff he was. In the event it did not happen; she rang to say, like him, she was stuck with extra business, had been forced to go north to Berwick and was likely to be there until late the following day. She did not arrive home until late and she was tired: there was no opportunity for talk.

By the end of the week the stiffness and soreness had eased and there seemed no point in talking to her about it.

At the weekend she asked him whether he'd had any further thoughts about the purchase of an interest in Martin and Channing. He said he hadn't, but would be interested to meet the senior partner in the firm when he visited them at Sedleigh Hall.

She told him it had all been arranged. He shot apparently, so she'd arranged a small group to go out on the moors. Eric excused himself from the shoot. A little sharply, Anne asked him whether he would nevertheless be at the dinner-party. Eric replied that he would: he was interested in making the acquaintance of Leonard Channing.

* * *

The senior partner in Martin and Channing was a little above middle height and about sixty years of age. His features were patrician, his nose narrow, his lips too thin to enable him to smile easily. His dark eyes had the confidence that came with dealing with other people's money and holding balances of financial power; his fingers were slim and long, with the suppleness of a pianist. The dinner had been decreed formal and his dinner jacket was immaculately cut, his tie the right shade of blue against the fashionable pale colour of his shirt. He spoke easily and charmingly; his manners were polished and his turn of phrase elegant.

He regarded himself as a man of the world and one with the experience to carry off any social situation. Because he held himself in such regard, Eric guessed, he would be held in that regard by others. He would be a tough man to bargain with, used to winning arguments.

What Eric found slightly disturbing was that he seemed already to have found an accord with Mark Fenham.

The young solicitor had met Leonard Channing several times in business meetings; of that Eric was aware. He was somewhat surprised to realize, nevertheless, that Mark Fenham seemed dazzled by the merchant banker. They used first names, and Fenham saw nothing patronizing in this; perhaps he was unaware of the nuances that would lead Channing to refer to others in the party, like Eric, by their surnames. A typical piece of English mannered snobbishness, of course, but indicative of something.

That something could mean that Channing believed Fenham was no problem; he could be manipulated.

Not that he seemed to give a second thought to Eric Ward. While he was not entirely dismissive, he clearly regarded Eric as lightweight, and not seriously involved in the future relationships between Martin and Channing and Anne Ward. It could have been that he was basing his attitude upon information and prejudices fed to him by Mark Fenham, but Eric was not fool enough to believe so entirely: Leonard Channing had looked at Eric Ward, talked briefly to him, measured him against the background he had been given by Mark Fenham and then, clearly, had dismissed him as someone of no real consequence.

Eric understood how the man might reach the conclusion, but was irritated, nevertheless. It led him, after dinner, to play a more positive role in the conversation than he had intended.

The members of the party had been well chosen, and equally well briefed. The shoot in the morning had been followed by a light lunch and the opportunity to relax, bathe, and stroll around Sedleigh Hall. Dinner had been taken relatively early but after the brandy most of the party had slipped away, murmuring their goodbyes. Leonard Channing had intimated he would need to get back to London early on the Sunday, so the opportunity for a last discussion, before formalities were headed for, would be after dinner.

Mark Fenham was there, with Channing and a little man who seemed to act in a personal capacity to the banker, Anne, Eric and the accountant Hoskins. Eric listened while various possibilities were discussed and the general area of agreement was hammered out.

Much of it, he felt, was stale ground. Fenham would have prepared most of the positions, discussed them with Channing or his people, and was now heading merely for confirmations. Eric was not sure Anne was aware of it; he himself saw certain lines along which the discussion was moving.

With Anne's permission, Channing had lit a cigar. He leaned back in his chair, enjoying the smoke, and he gestured towards the young lawyer in an expansive gesture. 'I've been impressed, Mrs Ward, by your adviser here. I won't say that when we met he showed me he had much more than the right *connections*, but I didn't know then that he had such a wise head on his shoulders. Morcomb Estates is lucky to hold him. I'm sure there would be other lucrative possibilities open to him elsewhere.'

Fenham laughed. 'It's kind of you to say so, Leonard. Maybe I didn't drive hard enough bargains with you.'

Leonard Channing's thin lips stretched to allow a smile. 'I wouldn't say that, exactly. I got the impression, when we were discussing business, that there were occasions when *I* was being stretched. And I'm not used to that situation. No, as I see it, Mrs Ward, Mark here has the capacity to seize a main chance when it arises, without loss to his clients and to obtain maximum advantage for his employer. He'll go a long way.'

'Into merchant banking, maybe?' Eric asked quietly. There was a brief pause. Leonard Channing was still smiling as he turned his head to glance at Eric, but the smile was a fixture, meaningless. 'I'm not certain I understand you, Ward.'

'Do you think Mark would find a place in an acceptance house, with his talents?' Eric asked innocently. He was aware of Anne staring at him, her brows knitting as she detected the line he was paying out to the merchant banker.

Leonard Channing's smile faded and he looked serious.

He nodded slowly, as though giving the matter careful thought. 'I consider his talents are such that he could make a career for himself. — a successful career — in a finance house.' The smile came back, widening to seek an appreciative audience. 'The *right* house, of course.'

'Like Martin and Channing.'

Anne started to say something but bit it back. Channing stared at Eric. 'It has not been discussed, of course, but . . . well,

Martin and Channing is a sound house for a young man to make his way, if he has legal and financial acumen.'

'I merely ask the question,' Eric said pleasantly, 'because if you were considering offering Mark a place in Martin and Channing there might be a problem.'

'Problem?'

'Conflict of interest,' Eric said blandly.

There was a short silence. Mark Fenham was leaning back in his chair, his handsome head to one side as though straining to pick up nuances he had missed. Anne was sitting stiffly, staring at him as though she was puzzled, tense because she was uncertain which way the discussion was heading. The accountant Hoskins looked worried; only Leonard Channing and his henchman appeared entirely unruffled. 'I'm not certain in what area a conflict of interest argument might arise,' Leonard Channing said.

'Neither am I,' Mark Fenham added.

Eric looked at the young lawyer. Fenham had paled, and his mouth had an angry set to it. Eric shrugged, and smiled frostily at Channing. 'Well, let's put it like this. Mark is an employee of Morcomb Estates. In that capacity he must always act in the best interests of the company that employs him. He is presently negotiating with Martin and Channing, on behalf of my wife, with a view to an interest being purchased in the acceptance house. Now let's assume he then joins Martin and Channing in some capacity — or indeed, merely receives a retainer from them.'

'So?' Fenham asked, unable to remove the trace of belligerence from his tone.

'There's almost bound to be a conflict of interest — at least, *potentially.* The business run by Morcomb Estates in which you act as adviser, Mark — covers land, timber, property, and *shares.* In the matter of share dealings where would advice be obtained? Would there be any possibility of, say, an investment in an issue controlled or placed by Martin and Channing? Could you always be sure that the advice you were proffering Anne and her company would be only to their advantage, and not to the *other* company paying you: Martin and Channing?'

'The question would never arise,' Fenham said angrily. 'You couldn't prevent the *possibility*,' Eric replied. 'Of course, one way around the problem would be that if you were offered a place or a retainer with Martin and Channing you could simply resign from your position at Morcomb Estates.'

Anne shifted uncomfortably, shot a quick glance at Mark Fenham and then glared at Eric. He ignored her. 'The trouble with *that* situation is that there might be some doubt, if the matter arose,' he continued, 'whether my wife had been badly advised by you in the first place. I mean, there's the argument that you could have been advising her into a bad bargain in order to fix yourself up with a place at Martin and Channing.'

'Eric, you're going too far!' Anne said angrily.

Leonard Channing stubbed out his cigar with an exaggerated care. 'No, no, Mrs Ward, let's not get too excited. Your husband is raising ethical issues here. I don't think we should ignore them, or dismiss them out of hand. The fact that they have no basis in truth is irrelevant, of course, for I have offered no such position to Mr Fenham.' There was a slight, almost imperceptible movement of Mark Fenham's head; Eric caught the movement, but did not look at him as Leonard Channing continued. 'It's not for me to say, naturally, who might be chosen to represent Mrs Ward's interests at Martin and Channing. Do I take it, from the interest you now seem to be taking in the discussion, that you yourself would be coming forward?'

'That might be the case,' Eric said.

Channing glanced towards Anne; she was staring at Eric, her eyes widening in surprise. She said nothing, and after a moment Channing smiled thinly. 'Interesting . . .' he commented.

'Of course, if I were to be involved in such deliberations I would want to know a great deal more about the business side of Martin and Channing. Just where the larger part of your profits are generated, for instance.'

Channing waved his hand airily. 'Basic banking still pays the rent at most accepting houses,' he said,' and Martin and Channing is no exception. It's the least glamorous activity, of course—'

'The rest of your business?'

'A mixed bag. We undertake a certain amount of specialized work — packaging international credits, putting together commercial loans for houses which have the money but lack expertise to arrange business themselves. There's a certain amount of project finance too; we recently put together a quite complicated package to build a dam in Africa, though I must admit we tend to turn away from business in black Africa, where there's payment expected over fifteen years . . .' He made a wry face as though he had tasted sharp lemon juice. 'Politics can be very damaging to a sound financial deal.'

'You'll be tendering in fiercely competitive fields,' Eric suggested.

'In every race,' Channing admitted, 'there are winners and losers and we don't always win. But we pull in reasonable fees for our corporate finance services and advice. Some houses feel they are grossly underpaid for such services; we're not greedy and consequently pull in quite a bit of satisfactory business, albeit with tight margins.'

'And mergers and acquisitions?'

Channing nodded thoughtfully, his eyes sharper now as he watched Eric. The air of negligent ease had gone. 'Yes, we run along that road too. We haven't the best track record in that kind of business and there's no way we can match the kind of fees that some of the American bankers obtain. But we've managed merger and acquisition fees in excess of £250,000.'

'Have you ever initiated such business yourself?'

'No,' Channing said quietly, 'we haven't.'

'Or maybe elaborated upon someone else's initiative?'

'You're talking of rich fields, Ward, and considerable risk. Is that the kind you would wish to commit your wife's capital to, the kind of business where caution goes out of the window and you ride hard for what may be immense or non-existent gains?'

'I wouldn't choose to advise my wife what she does with her money,' Eric said coolly.

Channing's eyelids flared momentarily. There was frost in his voice when he asked.' But when it *is* invested . . . ?'

'I would want to ask certain pertinent questions, if they had not already been asked.'

Mark Fenham stirred in his chair uneasily, but Anne barely noticed. She was still staring at Eric and her anger was not gone. Even so, she was listening. Channing nodded slowly. 'I can guess at the kind of questions.'

'Can you? Do they include the issue of protection?' Channing's lips twitched in irritation. 'A house with the reputation of Martin and Charming—'

'Shouldn't get uneasy at the prospect of an investor asking for guarantees that a degree of control would be available over the operation of the investment business.'

'A *degree* of control, no,' Channing said reluctantly. 'A seat on the main board?' Eric asked swiftly.

'That's never been raised as an issue,' Channing said hurriedly, 'and would prove to be an unreasonable request in the short term.'

'You mean you would refuse it?'

'I see little point in talking hypothetically—'

'You mean it hasn't been asked for in the negotiations?' Channing stared coldly at Eric. Whereas earlier his glance had been dismissive it now held hints of calculation, as though he were weighing up an opponent. 'Details have not yet been worked out, but I'm sure amicable solutions could be reached.'

'A seat on the board of Martin and Channing?'

'I didn't say that.' Channing glanced at his henchman briefly, then looked back to Eric. 'There is little point in taking a seat on a policy-making board if one doesn't really know what is going on. You have already pointed out that Mr

Fenham, as an employee of Morcomb Estates, would seem to be facing problems of conflict of interest. The purchase of a share in Martin and Channing is to be undertaken, I understand, not as part of the Morcomb Estates business but rather out of Mrs Ward's . . . personal finances.'

He glanced at Anne. 'That is so,' she said in a small voice. 'So if we were to talk about . . . representation, you would be able to nominate someone you trust . . . and who has the necessary understanding of the way we work.'

There was a challenge in the air and it was to Anne. She stared at Charming for several seconds, not understanding, and then she looked at Eric. He had refused till now to get involved in her business, refused to take part in Morcomb Estates. He had beaten his own track, down at the Quayside, and she had been angry and frustrated. But now, in a manner she clearly found bewildering he had chosen to challenge Leonard Channing, and Channing, in his turn was throwing a gauntlet down at her feet. *Trust*, he had said, and *understanding*.

The tension grew in the room as she sat silently, staring at Eric. Then, surprisingly, overconfident, Channing overplayed his hand. 'A company lawyer, of course,' he said, 'might be acceptable to us, but one in a general practice could not be expected to have the . . . ah . . . necessary background and expertise . . .'

Anne's glance flickered briefly over Charming and then she stared at Eric again. He was calm. It was her decision. He had not stated his position, but by inference it was there in front of her. The question was in her eyes but he would not answer her openly: Channing had used the words 'trust and understanding' and he had also now intimated that in his view Eric Ward was not the man to represent Anne's interests in Martin and Channing. A company lawyer like Mark Fenham should be first choice.

But Anne was asking the question in her eyes and he held her glance.

She was nothing if not loyal. 'My husband has my every confidence, Mr Charming,' she said slowly. 'He is not the company lawyer you suggest, but I am more than certain he would look after my interests admirably — and have a contribution to make to the firm itself.'

Channing's mouth registered annoyance; Mark Fenham's hands were very still and he sat rigidly, stunned by the turn of events. 'It is clearly up to you,' Channing said, 'though in the course of negotiations . . .' He bit off the words, then looked at Eric with cold eyes. 'We would not be able to agree, in the circumstances, to a seat on the main board.'

'I think that's something we can discuss in due course.'

Channing thought for a moment and then a slight, cynical smile touched his mouth. He nodded. 'Yes, I'm sure in our discussion we can reach a suitable . . . compromise.' He rose, abruptly. 'Mrs Ward, it's been an interesting, entertaining and most instructive day. You'll be aware I need to return to London tomorrow. I don't think there is much more we can usefully pursue this evening — we'll need to thrash out details later. So perhaps you'll forgive me now if I retire. I'm not as young as I used to be, and my best work is done in the mornings.'

His minion had risen with him; Mark Fenham now also rose, clumsily, seemingly somewhat disorientated still, and he also made an excuse to retire. After the good nights were said, and Hoskins had left the room in their train, Eric walked across to the drinks tray and poured himself a brandy. He looked at Anne. 'You'll join me?'

She was glaring at him, but the anger had been replaced by bemused curiosity. 'If you're celebrating something and you must be, to get on to the hard stuff — I will.'

He poured a somewhat larger brandy for her and walked across, handed her the glass and smiled. 'I quite enjoyed that.'

'Even though it means the end of your prized independence?'

His gaze met hers, levelly. 'It's a compromise, Anne, not a surrender.'

She frowned, uncertain, and shook her head in exasperation. 'Eric, I swear, there are times when I just don't know what the hell's going on inside your head. I never thought you would be prepared to work on this Martin and Channing thing. What the hell *is* going on?'

There was no time to tell her, even if, without reflection, he could have explained it to her satisfactorily. He heard a discreet cough behind him and he turned. Evans, Anne's butler, stood there, one hand on the door handle. 'I'm sorry to interrupt, madam,' he said, his Welsh rhythms breaking in on the words in a manner that was unusual.

'Yes?' Anne said.

'There's a gentleman called, madam. He would like to talk to Mr Ward.' The owlish eyes turned towards Eric. 'He says he's from the Northumberland Police.'

CHAPTER 2

The sickly smell of formaldehyde was strong in Eric Ward's nostrils. The mortuary assistant wore a white lab coat with stains on one narrow lapel. His eyes were blank and uninterested, his attitude listless. There was nothing in his care which had any connection with life: he regarded his charges as items, slabs of meat. It was a defensive mechanism Eric could understand, even though he was always slightly angered by it.

The police constable with him was young, and slightly green at the gills. He stood to one side while the assistant identified the relevant tag. He was shivering slightly; it could have been from the cold.

The assistant drew back the sheet. The police constable came forward. For a moment Eric thought the man was going to gag, but the words struggled out. 'Do you . . . recognize the man, sir?'

Recognition by his best friend would have been impossible. The body was swollen, puffed and putrescent with the immersion in seawater. The face was bloated, and crabs, or fish, had nibbled away at the flesh. Eric shook his head.

'There are no identifying characteristics you can point to?' the young constable persisted, trying to do his job and sweating in the cold air as he tried to control the impulses of his stomach. 'No,' Eric said shortly and turned away.

Silently the assistant covered the corpse, and the police constable hurried along behind Eric. At the door he pushed past him. 'Would you come back out to the car now, sir?' They drove swiftly away, back into Morpeth. Eric was silent in the back seat. Gusts of night air swept in on him as the constable breathed deep: the driver had edged away from him and the odour of formaldehyde which still clung to his uniform.

They parked in the yard behind the police station and Eric was escorted into the main building and up the stairs to the interview room. He was offered a cup of tea but declined it. He waited. Fifteen minutes passed before the constable in attendance straightened and the door behind Eric opened.

'All right lad, you can shove off.'

Eric knew the voice.

Detective-Superintendent Mason lowered himself into the seat facing Eric across the plain wooden table. His thick black hair was still springy, but greying heavily at the temples and his moustache was stragglier than Eric remembered, drooping in discontent at the corners of his mouth. The sleepy pouches under his eyes emphasized the gloomy cynicism that affected Mason; his blotchy skin sagged over his fleshy face and he glared at Eric with ill-concealed dislike. He was a muscular, short-tempered man whose attitudes and behaviour Eric had criticized in the old days, when they had both been on the beat. The scars from that relationship had remained, unhealed, and had indeed been opened again from time to time in the intervening years when their paths had crossed professionally.

'So,' Mason began heavily, 'not the best time of day.'

'Couldn't it have waited?' Eric asked.

'If I got to wander around in the middle of the bloody night and your name comes up, you think I'm not going to haul you out, too?' Mason sneered.

'Why has my name come up? And in what connection?' Mason glowered at him, old resentments seeping to the surface. He shook his heavy head. 'Trouble with you, Ward, you never learn. When you started as a solicitor you put all your police connections behind you: and you've forgotten, seems to me, that it's coppers who ask questions, not bloody lawyers, in your position.'

'And what position am I in?' Eric asked calmly.

'Curious one, I tell you that.' Mason leaned back in the chair and delved in his jacket pocket for a battered packet of cigarettes. He shook one out, lit it and smoked gloomily, staring at Eric through the drifting blue smoke. 'Got a capacity for getting into trouble, haven't you?'

'I'm still waiting to hear what this is all about.'

'The mortuary bring back any memories?'

'I don't know why I was taken there.'

'Didn't recognize the character we got on ice there, then?'

'I don't know why you expect that I should.'

'Little birds, little birds . . .'

'Now look, Mason—'

'No, you look, Ward. Don't get uppity with me. You always tried to make out you were so bloody superior, and now you're a flaming solicitor you're convinced of it. But you don't rate with me, you never have, and I freely admit it gives me a certain satisfaction to haul you out in the middle of the night to ask you some pertinent questions.'

'About what?'

'About Peter Knurling.'

Eric paused, eyeing the policeman carefully. 'I don't know anyone of that name.'

'No?' Mason jeered. 'Rings no bells for you?'

'None whatsoever.'

'Well, as you'll have gathered after seeing the recent deceased he's spent some time in the river. We fished him out of the Tyne some days back not far from J arrow Slake. Not that he entered the water there, of course: the tide will have pulled him down to the sea, down past Low Walker and Hebburn. First news we got, in fact, was from the river police station at Old Staiths. They got a report of something bumping about near the landing, but it was dark, they couldn't find it, and fifteen hours later it had travelled as far as the Slake. Took us a few days to identify him, then.' Eric waited, but Mason was silent, staring at him with a lopsided, unpleasant grin. 'Where do you think he entered the water?' Eric asked at last.

'Can't be certain, but we got some ideas. Based on solid investigative work, of course.'

Investigative work, as far as Mason had been concerned in the old days, had consisted of taking a youngster into a dark alley in Newcastle and battering his head against the wall. Eric waited.

'Funny thing, really, how nosey people are. Take this character who came to see us few days ago. Used to be in the Special Police, always sticking his nose in ever since, even though he hasn't been active in ten years. He gave us some information. Very useful. Led us to you.'

'How do you mean?'

'What's your connection with the *Gloria*, berthed on the Quayside at Newcastle?'

'Connection?' Eric thought for a moment. 'No real *connection* . . . I hold a retainer from Craig Lynch Marine Insurance, and they hold a bottomry bond on the *Gloria*. The bond was dishonoured and I acted for them in its impounding. As far as I'm aware she's still berthed at the Quayside — or was until the weekend, anyway, because I saw her there. The case is still pending, but I've had nothing to do with her since—'

'Since you stuck the notice on her mast?'

'That's right.'

'That's a lie.'

'Mason—'

'This character I told you about, the nosy ex-Special Police guy — he happened to be parking his car on the

Quayside couple of weeks back. He says he saw someone coming off the *Gloria.* It was dark and he wouldn't have paid much attention, but there were no lights aboard and this feller coming down the gangway, he was staggering or something. So our friend went up to him, asked him if he needed help, and got a pretty short answer. Suspicious like, he then hung around. He watched the guy off the boat go to a car, drive away. He took the car number.'

Eric was silent, waiting.

'He didn't leave it that, of course,' Mason continued. 'Not our ex-Special Policeman. Public-spirited character. He scanned the papers, just in case. And at last, when the *Journal* published a news item about a body being fished out of the Tyne he came running around to us. There might be a connection, he said. So we checked. The car number was yours. And dammit, we find some other interesting information. The skipper of the *Gloria* — he's gone missing. And from papers in the corpse's pocket-waterproof wallet, fortunately — we can make the link.'

'How did he die?' Eric asked.

'Painfully, my friend. He'd had a knife twisted in his gullet before he drowned. So now what do you say? Don't tell me you want to talk to a lawyer.'

Eric hesitated, thinking hard. 'I was on the *Gloria* one evening a couple of weeks ago—'

'What the hell were you doing there? Had you already fixed the notice? You wouldn't be doing that in the dark, dammit!'

'Take it quietly, Mason, and *listen.* I'd placed the statutory notice and had been working late in the office. I ate in town but had left my car near the office. When I drove away I thought I saw a light on the *Gloria.* I went to investigate—'

'*Hah*!'

'I thought it might have been someone trying to slip the *Gloria* out to sea, beyond the jurisdiction.'

'That your business?'

'Strictly, no, but having seen the light, I went aboard—'

'And you and Knurling had a jar of rum together and then things got out of hand—'

'I was attacked, Mason.'

'You what?'

'I called out, heard no one aboard, but when I reached the wheelhouse there was someone there behind the door. He struck me, I went down, and he got off the *Gloria* quickly.'

'I'd have waited to finish the job,' Mason glowered. 'This is a tall story you're telling me, Ward.'

'It's the truth.'

'You report it?'

'No.' Eric hesitated. 'I thought it was probably some youngster from one of the Tyneside gangs along Scotswood, lifting whatever he could find from the impounded boat. There was nothing there of value to steal, the below decks were secured, and I guessed the kid was scared, belted me and got the hell out of there.'

'That doesn't explain why you didn't report it. You didn't tell anyone?'

'There seemed no point,' Eric replied lamely. 'Didn't you even tell your wife?'

'She . . . she was away at the time. When she got back . . . there were other things to think of.'

Mason stubbed out his cigarette viciously. He folded his hands over his stomach and glared at Eric. 'Thin. Very thin.'

'It's the way it was.'

'And now? Now we know the skipper was knifed and dumped into the Tyne, maybe from the deck of the *Gloria*?'

'All I saw was a flash of light on the deck. I went aboard. Someone hammered me. I saw nothing; could identify no one.' Eric paused. 'That's all there is, Mason.'

'Not quite.' Detective-Superintendent Mason was silent for almost a minute. He stirred restlessly. 'You ever meet this guy Knurling?'

'No.'

'But you knew he was skipper of the *Gloria*.'

'No. My concern was with the vessel, through Craig Lynch Marine. I didn't know the names of the crew or other personnel involved.'

'So, naturally, you wouldn't have been aware that Knurling wasn't his real name?'

The silence grew around them as Eric made no answer. At last, Mason leaned forward, elbows on the table, thrusting his face nearer Eric's. 'The bugger was travelling under false papers, man,' he said. 'False documents, false master's ticket, the lot. That *costs*, you know. Not easy to get forged sea papers.'

'Do you know what his real name was?'

'We do. Mueller. Karl Mueller. He had lodgings in Felling. Found his passport there. The name familiar to you?'

'No.'

'Ward, all I'm getting from you is negatives.'

'That's all I have to give.'

'So you know nothing about Mueller or his movements; you've never come across the name Peter Knurling; you've no idea why he should change his name; you know nothing about the way he died; you can't *imagine* why he should have been killed, and you've certainly no idea who would have killed him — although you yourself got mugged on the deck of the *Gloria*. I suppose you don't even know anything about the voyage of the bloody ship, either.'

'Nothing,'

'You know sod — all about anything, that's about the size of it,' Mason muttered.

'Correct.'

Mason rose abruptly to his feet, towering over Eric and sending the chair crashing down behind him. 'You know me, Ward, I can be a violent man when I'm crossed. And I'm feeling crossed right now. Maybe you really do know nothing about this killing, but you're too close to the heart of it to let me feel comfortable. I don't like your story of the incident on the deck of the damned ship, but if that's all it was, and if you really are clear, then stay that way — *well* clear! But if you do know anything, if you're holding anything back on some mistaken crap about lawyer's privilege or something, I warn you, I'll break every bone—'

'Mason,' Eric said icily, 'you're not talking to some kid in a back alley now.'

Mason's eyes glittered with uncontrolled malice. 'Get the hell out of here,' he snarled.

* * *

As he made his way down the steps to the main entrance Eric glanced at his watch. It was almost three in the morning. He stopped at the duty room and asked if he could make a phone call. He rang Anne, and told her not to worry, he was on his way back. He requested a police car; there was a short delay. While he waited, he heard a voice in the corridor. It was one he knew from the old days.

Harry Parks was thirty-five now and had only recently been promoted to detective-sergeant. He'd been a raw recruit when Eric had taken him under his wing: they had always got on well together. When he saw Eric emerge from the duty room his boyish face creased into a grin. 'Eric! I heard you'd been pulled in, but I thought you'd gone.'

'I'm waiting for a squad car.'

Harry Parks nodded, glanced sideways, and then drew Eric a little way down the corridor. 'I heard Mason dragged you in. It was on the cards that as soon as he heard it was you, he'd jump in on it personally.'

'There's never been any love lost between us,' Eric agreed.

'So how are you mixed up in it?'

Eric explained. 'It's purely accidental, but Mason would love to hang something on me. What information do you have on the murdered man, anyway?'

Parks shrugged. 'Not a lot. And I got a feeling we're never going to get much. We've been on to Interpol, of course, but so far there's nothing. The voyage of the *Gloria* seems innocent enough—'

'There's been some bond trouble, a lien on the ship once the cargo was sold,' Eric interrupted.

'So we gather. But that doesn't seem to link up in any way. Ship's papers are OK, cargo manifest in order . . . it's just this guy has false papers, picked up the ship on the last leg to England and got himself knocked off in the Tyne. Why the hell didn't he wait to have it done somewhere else?'

'What about his passport?' Eric asked.

'In the name of Karl Mueller. Well-travelled, as you'd guess. Latest stopovers seem to have been in France, Spain and Switzerland. We're particularly checking the last. What's a sailor up to in Switzerland?'

'Your guess is as good as mine.'

'Occasionally better. Eric, good to see you. Keep in touch. And don't get involved in this kind of mucky business, hey?' It was not a matter of choice, Eric thought.

* * *

They had never found the body of William Jobling.

A hundred and thirty years previously he had had the privilege of being the last man gibbeted in England. They had trundled his remains along the South Shields turnpike to Jarrow Slake, encased the body in iron bars and covered it in pitch. They'd hoisted the body on to the twenty-foot-high gibbet: founded in a stone weighing one and a half tons, its height meant that the corpse would be displayed even at high water.

Within three weeks local pitmen, of whom Jobling had been one, spirited away the body under cover of darkness, so that it would not endure the humiliation of the gibbet for a crime arising out of the pitmen's strike. Rumour had it that the corpse had been buried at sea, or under the walls of the ancient monastery at Jarrow. It was never recovered.

It was years since Eric Ward had stood at Jarrow Slake and the scene was every bit as desolate as he remembered

— more so, perhaps, now that the dry docks at his back were deserted and the shipyards beyond Tyne Dock empty and quiet, rusting gantries gaunt against the dark morning sky.

A cold breeze ruffled the grey surface of the Slake as he stood on the jetty, looking out towards where the river police would have picked up the body of Karl Mueller. A few aimless ducks bobbed dispiritedly on the surface but there were no more than half a dozen waders to be seen among the shore rocks: Jarrow Slake had been well chosen for a gibbet, and it was a sad place for a man to end his days.

It was only curiosity that had drawn Eric down to the Slake. He was on his way to London, had an hour to spare in Newcastle, so had instructed the taxi-driver to take him across river to the Slake. The man was watching him now, sitting in his car on Slake Road. He would be puzzled: Jarrow Slake was no one's idea of a beauty spot.

Anne had been puzzled too, when she had asked him why he hadn't told her of the attack on board the *Gloria*. It had been difficult to explain: his silence had been occasioned in part by a desire not to worry or frighten her, and also because he felt there would be little purpose in telling her. The chances of finding his assailant from among the Scotswood gangs would have been remote and he had no intention of wasting the time of the Newcastle police. The matter had only taken on a different complexion when he had learned of the murder of Karl Mueller. It was perfectly possible that Eric had come close to the killer: he might well have disturbed the murderer when he had boarded the *Gloria*. Whether he had been searching for something on board, or merely checking with his flashlight to ensure that Mueller was dead in the water was a matter for conjecture.

He had been able to turn Anne aside from such anxieties by talking about the deal with Martin and Channing.

Just what *did* make you change your mind?' Anne had asked him.

Again, the answer was not an easy one. 'I suppose the argument we had that evening about Mark Fenham made me sit back and take stock. I've never made any secret of the fact that I need to make my own way—'

'It was an understanding we reached,' she agreed, 'without its ever being really discussed.'

'But I suppose I was taking the whole thing too far, in my insistence that I should not get involved with Morcomb Estates. Certainly, I would never want to be a director of your company: you run the whole thing perfectly well without my interference. But it's another matter to stand back entirely, and offer no help.'

'And Mark?' she asked quietly, but with a light of mischief in her eyes.

Eric laughed. 'All right, maybe there was an edge on that account also. But I didn't want a quarrel and . . . well, although I was reluctant to interfere, I got the impression Mark was getting a bit too *close* to the whole thing.'

'I'm not certain what you mean.'

'I think he was losing some of his objectivity, and that's dangerous in a lawyer. Besides, you have to remember, I'm expecting you to support me in my old age, and how will you manage that if you enter into rash business ventures?'

'A share in Martin and Channing can hardly be regarded as a rash business venture.'

And she was right. The opportunity was a good one. When he had seen the papers that had been prepared for Mark Fenham Eric was forced to agree that the financial base for the acceptance house was sound, its track record impressive, and its financial packages well researched. He had made inquiries among contacts in the North and in London and it was clear the firm was highly regarded.

The curiosity was that Martin and Channing were so prepared to countenance the investment from Anne Ward. Most deals of this nature were based on contacts within the financial world: the old boys' network was utilized, with families buying in on the basis of their status and social circle. Eric had managed to get no answer to that question. Anne's was new money, and money was always welcome but there was plenty of old money around for the asking. So why had Leonard Channing been so interested, and prepared to agree the investment?

Eric had his own theory about it. Channing was now in his sixties. He had dominated the firm as his father had before him. He had done all he had planned to do, perhaps, and it was time he planned for the day when he could take capital out of the business. There was the possibility Martin and Channing *needed* fresh money, cash that would not be tied up in fifteen-year investments, building projects that would not give an immediate return of the kind Channing might want in retirement.

Mark Fenham's approach on behalf of Anne Ward would have given Leonard Channing the chance he was looking for. An injection of a considerable nature, with few strings attached; a source of finance from someone new to the money game; a malleable, inexperienced legal adviser with no background in investment banking; the chance to offer a deal in which Channing and his partners would be giving little away.

And that's the way it would still be, unless Eric could tie things down to produce a better situation for Anne. One thing was in his favour: the City now knew of the proposed investment, and Channing would not wish it to blow up in his face. He could lose financial credibility and that was the business he was in: credibility. If the deal collapsed, rumours might start flying around and no financial house could afford that in the short run.

It was the only card Eric had to play, he thought, as he walked back from the jetty at Jarrow Slake and instructed the taxi-driver to take him to Newcastle Station.

* * *

The offices of Martin and Channing were not given to vulgar ostentation. They were housed in a drab, elderly building which made no effort to sell itself or parade its solid virtues.

Eric Ward entered the main doors and found himself in an entrance hall with a plain counter. He was escorted to a lift that seemed to have been designed for packages rather than people and clearly did not cater for casual visitors.

The waiting-room to which he was shown contained small circular tables and uncomfortable easy chairs. The annual report of Martin and Channing was carefully placed on each table: it proved to be a meagre document, containing no full-colour views of Lake Geneva, or flaring oil burners, or grey-suited men with handsome profiles talking earnestly down telephones while behind them a boardroom world waited expectantly. The acceptance house obviously regarded discretion as a major asset and recoiled from publicity or gimmickry.

The secretary who sat at the desk near the door also seemed to regard silence as a commercial asset. Perhaps it was company policy not to talk to strangers.

A bulky man in a blue suit entered after a little while; he had iron-grey hair and a smile to match. He nodded at Eric, introduced himself as Alan Scholes and led the way into the room beyond. The secretary managed a faint smile as they walked past.

Leonard Channing was already in the room. He was seated at the head of the oval table which dominated it. It was covered in green cloth and set with six cut-glass tumblers. Beside each glass were a notepad and a sharp pencil. In the centre of the table was a tray with a crisply white cloth on which had been placed two bottles of Malvern water and one of Perrier water.

Channing was not alone.

Scholes advanced apologetically. 'Ah, Leonard, our new friend was waiting outside and I thought you would probably have just about finished your discussion.'

Leonard Channing was frowning slightly, as though he would have preferred Scholes to have waited before bringing Eric in but he made light of it, turning to Eric as the two men with him rose to their feet. 'Ward, glad to see you. Ah . . .

you won't have met our two friends here. They are directors of the Storcaster Syndicate, an insurance business with whom we have dealings from time to time.' As he said it, something happened to his eyes, a hint of sudden amusement. Then it was gone as he returned to introduce the two men. 'This is Mr Daniels.'

'Phil Daniels,' the man said and extended his hand. There was a slight Bostonian accent but there were more cosmopolitan tones recognizable as Eric listened to the conversation that ensued. Daniels was square-built, muscular in shoulder and upper body, and Eric guessed he would be active in his leisure life. A reference to sailing and water-skiing eventually emerged in the discussion to confirm his suspicion. The second director of Storcaster was introduced as Saul Berckman. He had dark hair and heavy eyebrows, under which piercing eyes seemed to question intensely, missing nothing. His skin was swarthy, flawed on the cheekbone by a scar whose lividity suggested it was recent. Though he continued to listen closely to the discussion that continued with Leonard Channing, his eyes strayed from time to time in Eric's direction. There was a slight frown on his face, the dogged insistence upon solving a problem.

Eric's attention wandered. The antique clock on the far wall was precisely three minutes fast. To that extent, Martin and Channing looked to the future. As if to counterbalance this, the glass-fronted bookcase beside Eric contained curtains, carefully drawn across inside the glass as though to protect its contents from the gaze of the curious. The room had a faintly musty air; Eric suspected it might even have been deliberately cultivated. Modern financial business could feel so much more secure in an atmosphere of old-established dust.

He looked up. Saul Berckman was staring at him. The glance slipped away as Leonard Channing rose to his feet. 'Well, gentlemen,' he was saying, 'I won't pretend that the occasion is one of the happiest we have experienced, but you have my assurance that Martin and Channing always meets its obligations. Now that the papers have been released and the investigations concluded I feel certain that an accommodation can be arranged. It was good of you to call in; I always feel matters can be dealt with so much more effectively that way.' He was extending his hand. Gravely, he shook hands with Phil Daniels and Saul Berckman. In turn, they said goodbye to Scholes and Eric.

'I trust we'll meet again,' Daniels said as he shook hands, smiling.

Saul Berckman was standing just behind him. 'I have a feeling that when we do, it'll be for the third time,' he said.

Eric raised his eyebrows. 'We've met before?'

'I think so,' Berckman said thoughtfully. 'I've been watching you — I feel certain we've been at some meeting together, somewhere.'

'Well, let's hope any further acquaintanceship will prove profitable,' Leonard Channing said cheerfully.

Eric glanced at him. Channing had a sly smile on his face, in spite of the malicious glitter in his eyes. He was enjoying some joke of which Eric was unaware. The only consolation was that the men from Storcaster were clearly not in on it either.

When they had gone, Leonard Channing sat down with a sigh. 'Bad business,' he announced, 'but not a damn thing we can do about it.'

'You underwrote them?' Scholes asked. 'It wasn't a contract I negotiated.'

'We underwrote them,' Channing said bitterly, 'and it's going to cost us. Ward, let me warn you: steer clear of marine insurance if you can. Not that we can,' he added gloomily.

'Significant amount?' Eric asked.

'In marine insurance, *all* amounts are significant. However,' Channing went on more briskly, 'we're not here to discuss our liabilities or the extent of our business in marine insurance. I've asked Scholes to come in with you so that we can deal with the final details of our agreement. He's prepared the drafts for our approval. You have full authority of Mrs Ward, of course?'

'I have.'

'Well, let's get down to business.'

The drafts were full and extensive. Scholes was clearly a company lawyer with considerable financial experience and the drafts he had prepared were watertight. Eric spent the next hour going over them with him, while Channing sat listening, occasionally interrupting, drumming his fingers lightly on the table, appearing distant but in fact listening carefully to each point raised.

At the end of the hour Eric sat back. As though on a signal, a young woman in a grey suit came in with a tray of tea. The china was delicate, with a faint tracery of pink roses, almost transparent. The tea was faintly scented, expensive and carefully chosen, Eric guessed, to suit the palate of Leonard Channing.

'Well, Ward, are you able to profess yourself satisfied?'

'The tea is excellent.'

Leonard Channing did not like being teased; there was a snappishness in his reply when he said, 'I meant satisfied with the terms of the arrangement we are prepared to make with you.'

'In broad terms, yes.'

'Broad terms only?' Channing permitted himself a ghost of a smile. 'In business language that translates as *dissatisfaction*.'

'In my terms, it means what I say. I'm broadly in agreement with all you propose. But there are just two points of detail.'

'What might they be?'

Eric thought for a moment. 'The first thing is, the date of commencement.'

'It's in the documentation,' Scholes pointed out.

'The proposal is that full implementation does not take place for another six weeks.'

'That is so.'

'The investment will have been finalized in two weeks.' Scholes glanced in Channing's direction. The senior partner nodded gravely. 'I think you have to appreciate our position, Ward. The investment will be made by your wife and shares thereafter taken in the profits — the considerable profits that accrue to Martin and Channing. But much banking is long-term business. Let's take a power station project, abroad. The government of the "exporting" country will guarantee most but not all the finance. In the UK, if we are to arrange a five million pound package we'd expect to have four million covered by the Export Credits Guarantee Department. There's a risk in raising such finance, nevertheless. We expect to be paid for that risk.'

'I understand that.'

'The point is,' Channing said softly, 'we have a number of outstanding projects in which we have taken varying degrees of risk. We expect — at the very least, *hope* — *to* make a reasonable return against that risk. But the investment that Mrs Ward now makes is, shall we say, rather late in the day for participation in those profits. Her money comes in, yes, but the risks have already been taken so it is only right that she should not benefit from the profits. We calculate that the necessary arrangements, in accounting terms, will have been completed within a month or so from the investment: after that proper participation can be undertaken.'

'I see . . .' Eric said thoughtfully. 'So on certain projects we will have no share of the profits. Tell me, will these projects be isolated in risk terms also?'

'I'm sorry . . .' Channing affected not to understand.

'If losses are sustained, they will not be set against the Ward investment. I mean, if it works in one direction, for profits, should it not also work in regard to losses?'

'Difficulties—'

'Can be overcome. I'll have to insist, Channing, that there be no time-lag between investment and participation. If there is, both profits *and* risk are to be excluded until the relevant date.'

There was a short silence. Channing stared at Eric, his mouth set tightly and an angry glow in his cold eyes. At last he nodded. 'See to it, Scholes. The date can be changed. Is that all you have to say about this point, Ward?'

'Only one more thing under that head. Our discussions are now reaching final stages. You have made various decisions — before discussions started, I mean — but you now have current business being raised. Decisions will be taken by you in the next few weeks which could materially affect the investment my wife is making. I think we need to be informed of those decisions.'

'It's been the custom in this firm for me to undertake the more delicate negotiations *personally*,' Channing said, a warning note sounding in his tone. 'Are you suggesting you would wish to . . . interfere in such negotiations?'

'I certainly have no desire to interfere,' Eric said doggedly. 'What we want is information about what deals you are contemplating, or working on.'

'Security is essential in many such negotiations,' Channing snapped. 'It could be prejudiced, damaged, good business washed away if loose talk—'

'Information,' Eric said coolly, 'is essential in this initial period. I'll guarantee security, but we must know what is happening, if our investment is to be protected.'

'Martin and Channing will do the *protecting*,' Channing said, anger staining his voice. He hesitated, staring at Eric with barely concealed dislike and then, abruptly, he nodded.

'If you guarantee the security, the schedules will be shown to you.'

Scholes breathed out audibly; the tension that had arisen in the boardroom was getting to him. Eric had the impression that Scholes had never seen Channing being given a rough time before; it was an experience new to him, and he wasn't exactly enjoying the experience. It could rebound on Scholes, possibly, when Eric Ward had left.

'So is that it?' Channing asked.

'I think it covers the operational matters, generally,' Eric said easily. 'It still leaves undecided, of course, the major issue I raised with you at Sedleigh Hall.'

Channing smiled foxily. 'Perhaps you could remind me.'

'A seat on the board.'

Channing's smile thinned at the edges, hardened. 'I regret to inform you, Ward, that your request is out of the question. I have discussed the matter with my other partners and it really is not possible. I must say that your other requests during this last hour have not been unpredictable: if I thought they would not be raised, perhaps that is to tell you that I have underestimated you in your bargaining powers. However, I'm afraid you overstretch yourself on the matter of a seat on the board of Martin and Channing. There is no question of our acceding to that.'

'It'll be a sticking-point, Channing.'

'And you calculate we can't hold out, possibly losing face and credibility in the City if this investment fails to go through.' Channing nodded. 'There is some strength in that argument. But let me put another to you. The City is a sensitive bird. Its flight is dictated by the merest breezes. A finance house is monitored carefully; the merest hint of weakness, and credibility can disappear. Let me suggest that there are some in the City who already question why we wish to take your investment. If we were to accede to your request of a seat on the board it might be seen by such persons as a recognition that you have forced your hand because we *need* money from Lord Morcomb's daughter. We *don't* need it, Ward: not that much. My partners are therefore adamant. No seat on the hoard. And you should see the logic of it. If you *were* to invest *and* get a seat on the board the resultant flurry could cut the value of your investment. Is that wise practice?'

Eric nodded thoughtfully. He could follow the logic of the argument. But it did not satisfy his instincts for ensuring Anne's investment was adequately protected. Additionally, he was beginning to recognize the cat in Leonard Channing. 'You will, in view of the pressure you knew I would exert, have discussed a compromise with the rest of your board.'

'All life is compromise,' Channing said, 'and so is business. Yes, we have a compromise to suggest.'

‘Which is?’

‘We have two subsidiaries. One is based in the North-East. We would give you a seat on the board of that subsidiary.’

‘Stanley Investments.’

‘The same.’

Slowly, Eric said, ‘At the moment, my understanding is that Stanley Investments is controlled from London; it has no independent board.’

‘It will have, once Mrs Ward invests in Martin and Channing. *You.*’ Channing smiled maliciously. ‘And that opportunity should excite you, Ward, surely — the chance to develop and extend the business acumen you undoubtedly feel you already possess.’

* * *

The package that he finally took back to Northumberland was the best he could have realistically hoped to achieve and it had one further bonus: it brought his relationship with Anne back on an even keel. She seemed relaxed, and loving, satisfied that he had seen fit to demonstrate his concern and love for her by sacrificing a degree of the independence she knew he needed, in order to help her over the Martin and Channing business.

As for Eric himself, he had to admit that the involvement projected with Channing and the Stanley Investments subsidiary in Newcastle stirred his blood: it was a new field a new venture that he knew would provide him with a challenge of a kind he had not faced before. He was not an entire novice in financial affairs, because it was his understanding of tax and finance law that had first brought him to the notice of Lord Morcomb at Sedleigh Hall, but it was another, and large, step to start working in the financial field through a merchant bank. It would not be a matter of applying his knowledge of tax matters: it would involve the development of his negotiating skills, of handling people, of walking the tightrope between acceptable and unacceptable financial risks.

It was a matter of a week or so before the arrangement with Martin and Channing could be established so Eric took the opportunity to take a few days' leave from the office. He paid a visit to the specialist in Newcastle to have a check-up on his eyesight and the results proved encouraging. He had not had a great deal of discomfort recently, and this pleased the specialist. Examination showed that there was no inflammation and the occasional use of drugs was arresting the condition.

'The prognosis seems pretty good. You're not getting any stinging or burning from the BP preparation? If so, we can transfer you to another proprietary which has a different vehicle.'

'No, there's no real problem,' Eric replied.

'Fine. Well, the trabecular meshwork seems fairly free, and the drainage of the aqueous through it isn't adversely affected. You're aware the condition can't be reversed and treatment has to be maintained, but I can tell you that the central vision hasn't been worsened: the condition has been arrested. But . . . remember, a normal life, and avoid tension, and problems. In other words, stay cool.'

When he took the good news back to Sedleigh Hall Eric suggested they spend a few days relaxing. Anne was only too happy to agree: Morcomb Estates had been taking up a great deal of her time, and with Eric busy in the Quayside office it seemed as though they had not had a great deal of time available for each other of recent months.

The days were spent riding in the hills, and walking across the fells on the northern boundaries of the estate. Anne was a more practised rider than Eric, and she knew the hills far better than he, but he was content to pace along behind her, follow her lead, and remember from time to time the first time he had seen her, riding down through the woods with the sunlight in her hair.

Mark Fenham came to dinner one of the evenings at Sedleigh Hall: he had some papers for Anne to sign relating to the management of Morcomb Estates, and he was also able to discuss with her the details of her father's will, now that the property was coming to her in total. The investments had been realized, and all was in order for the deal with Martin and Channing to go through.

Anne was careful enough, in Eric's presence, not to discuss the arrangements Eric had reached with Channing, and Mark Fenham himself did not allude to them. He was somewhat cool towards Eric, not offensively, but the constraint that was almost inevitable after their last meeting had now hardened, and although dinner was spent in sociable conversation, laced with business talk relating to the Morcomb Estates, it was with a certain sense of relief that Eric heard Fenham refuse an offer of accommodation for the night. He had business in Alnwick early next day, and thought it more sensible to return to his home in Morpeth.

When he returned to the Quayside office, Eric noted that the *Gloria* was still berthed on the river. Young Elias was able to bring him up to date on general office business, but Eric rang Tom Stevens, at Craig Lynch Marine Insurance, to find out what was happening about the impounding of the ship.

'We've had representations from the owners,' Stevens said, 'and it looks as though they might stump up against the claim we're making. You've had no correspondence so far?'

'Nothing's arrived here.'

'Mmmm . . . Things have got a bit complicated with the police swarming all over the bloody boat, as well. You heard about that, of course?'

Eric said he had. 'In fact, I can see they've still got someone on board. A token guard. You won't have to wait until their investigations into the death of the skipper are over, however, before you proceed with your claim.'

'*That* is a relief. The gossip we hear is that the fuzz has no idea where to start. The guy they fished out of Jarrow Slake was certainly skipper of the *Gloria* but the story is he was carrying false papers and no one really knows what the hell he was up to. He boarded, incidentally, in France. He wasn't there for the whole voyage.'

'A replacement, you mean?'

'That's right,' Stevens said. 'The whisper is that the skipper was taken ill, this guy shows up with appropriate papers and gets taken on, and away they go. But the question that's now being asked is whether it was a fix.'

'How do you mean?'

'All we get is the gossip, of course, but there's a story going the rounds of the waterfront that our dead friend actually had something to do with the mystery illness of his predecessor. There's a French newspaper report — interview with the previous skipper — where it's suggested the bloke was rendered *hors de combat* or whatever they say in French.'

'You mean drugged, to allow the replacement?'

'No details, old son, but something like that. But it's not something *I* can understand. I mean, who would want to leave sunny France to come to Tyneside, for God's sake?'

'There are worse places.'

'Not many!'

* * *

The police presence on the *Gloria* remained discreet but real during the next few days. A scattering of sightseers visited the Quayside berth each day, but once the novelty wore off the numbers decreased, and by the end of the week, when Eric was able to negotiate a settlement over the claim against the ship, the decision had been taken to withdraw the police guard. On the Saturday morning the statutory notice was stripped from the mast. On the midday tide on Monday, the *Gloria* slipped her moorings and set off for Tynemouth. Eric watched her go from his office window: she went with a minimum of fuss, observed by the occupants of one police car and a few small boys. As a *cause célèbre* on Tyneside the *Gloria* was finished. There was no information being made public as to why Karl Mueller had died, or who had killed him, or why he had been carrying false papers.

On Monday afternoon, Eric decided it was time he visited Stanley Investments.

The arrangements with Martin and Channing had been concluded the previous week, but Eric had not made any attempt to visit the office of the Newcastle subsidiary, nor to contact Reuben Podmore. He felt slightly uneasy about the prospect; he was not sure whether Podmore would yet have realized Eric Ward's involvement with Anne's investment.

He decided it was a confrontation he could no longer delay.

At three in the afternoon he walked up Gray Street and turned into the side street to enter the offices of Stanley Investments.

In the reception office at the top of the stairs there was a middle-aged woman seated behind the desk. Her hair was greying; she had a pleasant face with warm brown eyes and a controlled smile. She was dressed neatly and unostentatiously. Her desk was unlittered and she seemed efficient, but Eric wondered whether she had a great deal to do. The visual display unit on the microcomputer behind her was blank. He gave her his name.

Her eyes widened. 'Oh, Mr Ward, we've been expecting you.' She had a Durham accent, south of the Wear. 'I'm sure you can go straight in: Mr Podmore has been waiting for you.'

She rose and walked to the door to the investment manager's office, tapped on it and entered. There was a hurried, brief conversation inside and then she reappeared, smiling. 'Mr Podmore will see you at once, Mr Ward.'

Eric entered Podmore's office. He could not help contrasting it with the premises of Martin and Channing in Lombard Street. It was similar only in its lack of ostentation. But where Channing's premises had an elegance and style albeit somewhat spartan in taste — Podmore's office was worn, frayed at the edges in appearance, with a thin carpet, nondescript wallpaper, and narrow window. Eric advanced and put out his hand. Podmore, standing behind his desk, took it warily.

'Please, Mr Ward, take a seat. Sandra will bring in some tea, if you wish.'

'That would be most welcome, Mr Podmore.'

Eric took the seat facing Podmore across his desk. Podmore sat down slowly. He looked at Eric, his pale blue eyes holding shadows of disappointment, and his discontented mouth now marked with an added sadness. 'I'm glad you've found time to call, Mr Ward.'

'I came around as soon as I could,' Eric said evasively, uncomfortable at the way Podmore was staring at him. 'The last time we met,' Podmore said heavily, 'you had me at a disadvantage.'

'How do you mean?'

'I thought your visit was . . . unmotivated. I thought you were renewing an old acquaintance. I was not aware you had an interest in visiting me.'

'I asked you certain questions,' Eric replied. 'They must have shown you . . . and I did tell you I had a client who was interested in the background to merchant banking.'

That's not quite the same thing as admitting that the client was your wife, that you had a personal interest in merchant banking, and that your intention was to draw information from me regarding Stanley Investments, a subsidiary of a London merchant bank in which your wife was considering taking a partnership. Really, Mr Ward, I'm disappointed and not afraid to say so. I believe you took advantage of me; were not honest with me; attempted to obtain confidential information from me on the basis of an old-established acquaintanceship—'

'I think that's rather overstating the issue Mr Podmore. I admit I did not tell you my wife's connection with Martin and Channing, but I was doing no more than any solicitor would have done in protecting a client's interests — making inquiries about the viability of a business in which an investment was contemplated.'

'But I gather from my own inquiries, that Mrs Ward was not exactly a client of yours — rather, you have consistently distanced yourself from her business affairs. However I see little point in pursuing this conversational line. The matter is completed. Your wife has purchased her interest in Martin and Channing. You, I gather, are acting as her representative in the business. I have stated my concern and disappointment, and there it shall rest. The question now is what you wish to be done.'

'That depends.'

'On what?'

'On whatever advice you are going to give me.'

Reuben Podmore stared owlishly at Eric. His hand strayed up to caress his heavy jowls, as he considered the matter. 'My understanding of the situation is that for the first time a degree of independence is to be given to Stanley Investments. Up to this point of time affairs have been controlled from Lombard Street. Now, a separate board is to be established here in Newcastle to direct our business; you are the only member so far and you have freedom to make appointments as you wish. I'm not clear there is any place for me in this situation.'

'Why not?' Eric asked.

'I presume you will have nominees to appoint to your board, and advisers, which will make my position redundant.' He smiled reluctantly, as though he had made a private joke.

Eric shook his head. 'It hasn't been my intention to make you redundant, and at this stage I have no one in mind to appoint as adviser or member of the "board". The first thing is to discuss with you, and take your advice on, the main nature of the business Stanley Investments undertakes.'

Reuben Podmore's eyes narrowed. He stared thoughtfully at Eric for several seconds. 'The arrangement you reached with Leonard Channing . . . Did you discuss in any detail the operation of Stanley Investments?'

'The assurance I received was that the normal range of merchant banking activities was placed through the company.'

'In *these* offices, Mr Ward?'

'Leonard Channing—'

'The firm of Martin and Channing,' Podmore interrupted, 'took over this company years ago. At that time it was thriving. Situations changed. The premises were sold, the business moved to this address, and the whole thing developed into little more than an accommodation address.'

'A *what*?'

'It makes good sense to Martin and Channing. They use both their subsidiaries in the same way. I am the investment manager here, but I am not encouraged to seek new investments, or undertake new business. All business that comes our way is channelled through from Lombard Street. As you can see, there are virtually no staff costs, and overheads are low. We do very little work, and my title is little more than a cover for a job as a clerk.'

'You said it makes good sense to Lombard Street. How?'

'Tax. Write-offs. Publicity. It's quite a neat, inexpensive device that helps their corporate image considerably. The reason why we do no new business to speak of is that we are used as a dumping ground for embarrassing contracts. Martin and Channing are in the credibility market: they need to show a sound face to the world. Like every house, however, there are occasions when their judgement proves to be less than sound. There are times when payments have to be made, payments of some consequence; if too many of these items occur in the Martin and Channing balance sheet, some of their reputation might crumble. So, the answer is to use their subsidiaries to discreetly take on the burdens in *their* accounts, avoiding the bad publicity that might otherwise accrue to their main operation in Lombard Street. It's partly a tax avoidance scheme, and partly a face-saving exercise.'

'You mean that Stanley Investments is little more than—'

'A paper tiger, Mr Ward. I'm sorry to disappoint you, but your splendid new position, running the board of this company, will be nothing more than a mere sop to your vanity.'

The discreet tap on the door was followed by Sandra's entrance with the tea. She poured two cups; as she did so Eric sat back in his chair, thinking. They were not pleasant thoughts.

He had come back north from London believing he had won a battle of some consequence with Leonard Channing. He had thought he had outmanoeuvred the banker, had managed a deal which left Channing at the disadvantage.

In fact he had been manipulated, played at the end of a line. The 'compromise' Channing had agreed to at the end had been no compromise at all: a denial of a seat on the board of the parent company had been followed by the Stanley Investments offer, but it had in fact been worthless. Channing had been giving nothing away.

Eric had failed miserably. Anne's investment in Martin and Channing was safe enough, but the extra protection that would have been achieved by representation on the board had not been gained: Eric Ward had been bought off and Channing had made a fool of him. He recalled bitterly, now, the way a malicious smile had played around Channing's mouth during the negotiations. He had been aware of Eric's beliefs and had been enjoying the game. Another thought slowly seeped into Eric's brain.

'Profits,' he said slowly, after Sandra had left them. 'What are your net profits here in the North-East, Mr Podmore?'

'We're not in the business of making profits,' Podmore said quietly. 'We're here to make losses for Martin and Channing.'

So even the six-week delay had been a ploy on Leonard Channing's part. By insisting on an earlier date for completion of the agreement Eric might well have cost Anne money. She was committed, now, to accept current losses and risks as well as profits.

'What are your likely losses this year?' Eric asked.

'Considerable. Largely because of the contract with the Storcaster Syndicate.' Podmore frowned slightly, as though trying to remember something. 'Yes . . . you might recall, the day you called here to see me, two of their board members were here, discussing the issues with me. They went on to see Channing later, I know, but it's through Stanley Investments that the claims will be paid.'

There was a cold feeling in Eric's stomach. He really had been played for an inexperienced, arrogant fool. He now knew precisely why Channing had been amused. And why Saul Berckman, director of Storcaster, had stared at him, puzzled, wondering where they had met before. They *had* met; Berckman and Daniels had *seen* Eric Ward, here in the office of Stanley Investments, when he was arriving and they were leaving.

And Channing had known there was every chance they would meet again. In the off-loading of an expensive loss in a contract made with Storcaster.

'You say you're not encouraged to seek new business,'

Eric said flatly. 'That's right.'

'That must change.'

'More easily said than done, Mr Ward. It would be very much starting from scratch. Fifteen years' inactivity—'

'You're a subsidiary of Martin and Channing. You can trade on their reputation and credibility.'

'That's not the way it works,' Podmore protested. 'All decisions about new business are taken in Lombard Street. I have no authority—'

'You've *had* no authority,' Eric interrupted. 'You forget. Your words were that Stanley Investments have a *degree of independence* from Martin and Channing. Let's exercise that independence.'

'My authority—'

'Will stem from the new board of this company. I'm the only director of the board. I have power to appoint others. You will retain your status as investment manager, but we will together constitute the board. I'll make the necessary arrangements.'

Reuben Podmore was silent for a while. He had caught the anger in Eric's tone, and maybe guessed at the reasons for that anger. He waited, as though he was giving Eric time to cool down. 'It still isn't going to be that easy, Mr Ward. To build up confidence takes years. And assets—'

'We have the assets of Martin and Channing behind us. The days of this company as a paper tiger are over.'

'You're going too fast, Mr Ward.'

'I also read the financial news. I understand that the Deutsche Bank has announced that it wants to raise some two hundred million pounds for GADF, the West German machine tools company.'

Podmore blinked. 'That's so. The *Financial Times* ran a piece on it this morning. They're the leading all-purpose bank in the Federal Republic of Germany—'

'And GADF?'

'They're an expanding company. They've got considerable government contracts, their export earnings are high and their potential growth considerable.'

Eric considered for a few moments. 'How is the loan to be financed?'

'It will be through the Eurodollar market—'

'Eurodollars?'

Podmore sighed and pressed his fingertips together gently. 'Forgive me. There is no such thing, physically, as a Eurodollar. Legally, Eurodollars are US dollar credits owned and circulating outside the United States. They're the nearest thing the world has to an international currency—'

'Replacing the function sterling used to have?' Eric asked.

'That's right. Really, they're just dollars, ultimate claims against the US monetary system. They began to accumulate during the 1960s as deposits in European banks — so they're called Eurodollars. And nowadays the world's money market for bank borrowing and lending is, in effect, the Eurodollar market.'

'I see.' Eric frowned. 'But that means only commercial banks can play — the ones with the deposits.'

'Right. The *investment* banks don't have the deposits, but they come into the business by organizing large syndicated loans. So where borrowers don't want straight bank loans they issue interest-bearing bonds to investors. They borrow their Eurodollars in that way. By issuing Eurobonds.'

'And that's how this loan will be financed?'

'Precisely.' Reuben Podmore allowed a shadow of doubt to cross his features. 'I wouldn't say it's the best time for a Eurobond issue—'

'Will Martin and Channing be interested?'

Podmore pursed his lips and considered the question. At last he shrugged. 'It's possible. I think there are . . . risks. I wouldn't know what policy will be thrashed out concerning the issue, at board level.'

Neither would I, Eric thought bitterly. He nodded. 'All right. Get me all the details you can on the issue.'

'Forgive me, Mr Ward, but why are you interested?' Eric hesitated, uncertain how to answer. He shook his head doubtfully. 'It's just that, seeing the report this morning . . . I thought . . . well, maybe we could be doing some business there for Stanley Investments.'

'You can't be serious, Mr Ward!'

'Why not?'

'We have no financial credibility.'

'We have Martin and Channing behind us and—'

'Mr Ward.' Podmore raised a pudgy, admonitory hand. He opened the drawer of his desk and took out a file. He opened it; inside there were a number of newspaper cuttings and brochures, annual reports, statistics. He extracted several cuttings and handed them over to Eric.

'What are these?' Eric asked.

'That one is a commemorating of the Credit Suisse deal. The next one . . . that's the Redman rights issue. Then there's the Merrell Stephens bond issue, and the Oklahoma Sancerre issue . . . They're tombstones, Mr Ward.'

'So?'

'If you look down the list, Martin and Channing stand prominently on a couple of them, rather lower down on some of the others.'

'With the major houses appearing top left. Yes, you explained to me all about tombstones,' Eric said. 'So why are you showing these to me?'

'Because while Martin and Channing appear prominently on all those rights issues, nowhere will you find the name Stanley Investments. In the financial world we disappeared off the face of the earth years ago. We have no status, no standing. There's no way we can break into the magic circle when the parent company has been doing the tombstoning without mentioning the subsidiary.'

'This has been a common pattern?'

'For years.'

Eric thought it over for several minutes as he inspected the lists of names under the issues. He handed the papers back to Podmore. 'Nevertheless,' he said, 'get me all the details you can on the Eurobond issues.'

Reuben Podmore sighed. 'As you wish, Mr Ward. Is there anything else you require from me?'

Eric nodded. 'You have the papers relevant to the Storcaster Syndicate?'

'I have. It was an underwriting. The reason why Mr Berckman and Mr Daniels came to see me was to discuss some of the papers with me, since the loss adjustment was to be made through this company rather than through Martin and Channing.'

'Sluicing away the expensive losses again, is it?'

'That is so, I'm afraid.'

'Right, well, I'd better see what it's all about. Let me have the papers and I'll take them home with me to read.'

'It's all but wound up, Mr Ward. There was an arbitration hearing some weeks ago in London. The Commercial Court took a damages hearing two months ago. It's more or less all dealt with—'

'What's it all about?'

'The underwriting contract related to the loss of vessel and cargo in the Mediterranean. The ship was called the *Sea Dawn*.'

'I'll take the papers with me. When will you next be meeting the Storcaster Syndicate representatives?'

'Nothing is scheduled yet. I'm awaiting word from Mr Channing—'

'Well, in future you also wait for word from me.'

* * *

Anne was in town that day so he had arranged to meet her at the fiat before dining in the city. Eric went back to his office to deal with some outstanding matters, and then left for the fiat, taking the *Sea Dawn* papers with him.

When he arrived at the fiat in Gosforth he made himself a coffee and sat down with the information Podmore had given him. Anne wasn't due in until seven thirty so he had an hour or so to wait until she arrived. He would change and shower after she had started getting herself ready.

He checked through the file Podmore had presented to him. There was a copy of the arbitration award, together with some supporting affidavits. The judgement of the Commercial Court was also included, together with some actuarial evidence by way of affidavit. He browsed through them until he reached the awards statements. He grimaced: £330,000 in respect of the ship; £250,000 as cargo loss. It was quite a loss that Martin and Channing were handing over to the northern company to run through their books. True, Lombard Street would have to bear the actual loss, but Eric was already beginning to feel resentful that Stanley Investments should theoretically have to carry such burdens on paper. There was also the still-rankling feeling that he had been conned by Leonard Channing, bought off like a spoiled child.

He quickly read the judgement of the Commercial Court which detailed the facts of the loss of the *Sea Dawn* and her cargo. Time passed quickly. He was absorbed in the papers, and was hardly aware of the door opening and Anne coming into the flat.

She walked forward and kissed him on the cheek. He made no response.

'Well,' she snorted, 'that's no way to greet your nearest and dearest!'

Eric ignored her, concentrating on the papers in his hand.

She stared at him, shrugged and took off her coat, poured herself a drink and came across to sit on the arm of the easy chair. She put an arm around his shoulders. 'So what are you reading that's so interesting?'

He glanced up at her, frowning. 'These are the papers relating to the loss of a ship and cargo in the Mediterranean.'

'*Fascinating*! Did it just disappear?'

'No. It was holed, and sank after repair work was started on it.'

'This come in to you from Craig Lynch Marine Insurance?'

'No. From Stanley Investments.'

'Well, well, well.' She glanced at him, observing the frown that he still wore. 'So what's gripping your attention so fiercely? There are problems in the case?'

'Not so far as the courts seem to say. The issues have been arbitrated upon and adjudicated upon. It's more or less all over bar the shouting.'

'So what's—'

'It's this.' Eric extracted a sheet from the papers and handed it to Anne. She stared at it for several seconds. 'A list of names,' she announced.

'Crew of the *Sea Dawn*.'

'So?'

'Look at the name of the first mate.'

Anne checked down the list. 'Here it is. Mueller. Karl Mueller.' She frowned. 'I know that name. He's . . . he's . . .'

Eric nodded. 'He's the sailor the river police pulled out of the water the other week, at Jarrow Slake. Sometime skipper of the *Gloria*.'

CHAPTER 3

Tom Stevens was a craggy man with brown crinkly hair and a barrel chest. He was forty years of age, he had confided to Eric, and a Tynesider born and bred, but his ambition now was to get away from the North. 'Things have changed so much, man. The river's not what it was, the unemployment is shattering, almost all the shipyards are closed and the coal's nearly gone. I canna see a future for my kids — I got two, you know, and what's there for them up here? Why, you canna even get a piece of hake these days — it's only cod, or these fancy fish.'

The 'fancy fish' was sea bass and it had been served with all the trimmings. They were sitting in the restaurant at Marsdon Grotto. Drilled out of the solid rock and reached by a lift, its windows gave a splendid view of Mars don Rock, wind and sea-eroded and clustered with bird life, just fifty yards off shore. Eric listened as Stevens extolled the virtue of the hake his mother had cooked for him as a child, the white flesh, the triangular bone. 'Not that this is too bad, mind.'

Eric smiled. 'I'm glad to hear it.'

'Anyway,' Stevens said, pushing the plate aside, 'there's always the hope Craig Lynch will give me an overseas berth.'

'Is there much chance of that?'

'Well, they got an office in Madrid, you know: Craig Lynch is really a subsidiary of an American firm with interests in Europe. They set up in Newcastle maybe twenty years ago, really because of the Norwegian traffic. Though that's fallen off badly enough these days.'

'Even so, Craig Lynch does a lot of marine insurance,' Eric said.

'That's so . . .' Tom Stevens glanced warily at Eric and smiled. 'And I've been rabbiting on about my own problems. You'll not have invited me out here to the Grotto just for the pleasure of my company. Or even, knowing you, to try to wheedle some business out of me.'

Eric laughed and poured Stevens another glass of wine. 'True enough. The *Gloria* is all settled and I've no other business in hand with you but I'm not seeking any, particularly. Rather, the *Gloria* — and certain other transactions arising — have made me curious about the marine insurance business.'

'Highly specialized.'

'So I believe.'

'And a funny business entirely.'

'Why do you say that?'

Tom Stevens sipped at his wine and stared out at Marsdon Rock. 'I've been in the business, mainly with Craig Lynch, for about twenty years. Marine insurance, I very quickly discovered, isn't like other forms of cover.'

'How do you mean?'

'Well, if you look at other forms of insurance the parties enter a written document which in effect forms the basis of the contract. It's on the terms of that document that issues will be resolved. A marine policy is a different kind of thing again, in the sense that where problems arise, they're largely because of the imbalance of the knowledge between the parties to the contract. The horrible fact is, of course, that although the underwriter has to rely upon information given to him when he makes the estimates for the contract, the person giving him the information is the guy who's getting the insurance.'

'So?'

'Well, the facts upon which we have to compute the risk are really within the knowledge of the other guy, almost exclusively. We don't check them.'

'You mean when you're negotiating the contract of marine insurance you don't satisfy yourself as to the accuracy of the statements made to you?'

Tom Stevens shrugged. 'More or less. Look, under the Marine Insurance Act the assured party must disclose to Craig Lynch every material circumstance known to him. So, if he doesn't, he's getting a financial advantage over the company, isn't he?'

'That's so.'

'But maybe he goes further. Maybe he doesn't just withhold information to his detriment; maybe he actually misrepresents material circumstances during the negotiations. Such as the condition of the vessel in hull insurance, for instance. We had a case a while back where a guy didn't disclose the fact the bloody ship had excessive rhythmic vibrations and leaked like a sieve. There was actually a marine surveyor's report on that one which said she was unfit for use offshore, but he didn't disclose that to us.'

'But if you discover a misrepresentation, or a nondisclosure of a fact essential to the contract, that would allow you to avoid the policy?' Eric asked.

'That's so, and it's the case even if the act was fraudulent, negligent or merely an innocent mistake. We do get ignorant ones occasionally! But one of the most common frauds IS extremely hard to detect. That's over-insurance. You get an old tub that's fit only for the scrapyard; the owner takes out a mortgage on her, at a sum say four times the true value of the vessel, and then when the tub sinks he recovers quite a nice packet — maybe enough to buy a new boat.'

'You can't quibble over the amount payable on the policy?'

Tom Stevens stared at Eric for a few seconds. 'Don't tell me you've got something like this in your own backyard! Well, if one of your clients is getting his fingers burned it's none of my business. Fact is you *can't* quibble about the amount. The valuation expressed in the policy is final.'

'Subject to no exceptions?' Eric asked.

Tom Stevens waved his glass negligently, spilling a little of the red wine on the tablecloth. 'Damn . . . well, yes, there are exceptions. I mean, if there's been fraud or nondisclosure, or *gross* overvaluation, okay, you can do something about it. But otherwise, since it's a contract of indemnity and the valuation is stated in the policy, with the premium agreed, you're stuck with it.' He screwed his eyes up in thought. 'There was a case that settled it, sixty years ago. Unless you can actually produce hard evidence of overvaluation, the figure in the policy is binding.'

'I would have thought,' Eric said slowly, 'that when he enters a marine insurance policy, an underwriter like Craig Lynch would verify as much of the information given as could possibly be done.'

Tom Stevens nodded. 'Naturally. And some of us do just that. There are facilities — there's the *Lloyd's Register of Shipping*, for instance. You can also ask for recent condition survey reports on a vessel. You can ask to see the bill of sale where a vessel has recently changed hands. But all this takes time, my friend, arid time's money—'

'The loss is surely greater when you have to pay out on an overvalued ship.'

'Okay, but there are companies — and I'm not saying Craig Lynch is one — who don't do the checking they should. They work on a number of premises. In the first instance, maybe the ship won't go down. That's an acceptable risk. In the second place they calculate that since they can't get all the information easily, why bother? They simply agree the. Insurance and fix the rates high. They'll argue it's easier to pay losses thereafter than fight a claimant anyway. Particularly since any underwriter who's going to fight a claim — even if he knows it's fraudulent — faces two big hurdles.'

'What are they?'

'First of all the other guy *knows* all the facts and the company can only guess at them.'

'That's a problem.'

'Sure as hell it is,' Stevens said warmly. 'And the second thing is the overvaluation may well have been deliberately done with the intention that the owner will in due course scuttle the bloody vessel to claim the insurance.'

'What's the problem there?'

'Believe it or not, the scuttler has an advantage, other than being the only guy in possession of the full facts. When he makes his claim he can say the loss was due to *perils of the seas*.'

'And perils of the seas has a particular meaning?'

'You got it in one. It amounts to — the words are engraved on Craig Lynch hearts — *fortuitous accidents or casualties of the seas*. And the law says the burden of proving a ship was *not* lost in this way lies upon the underwriter. In other words he's got to *prove* there was some fiddle going on.'

'That could be difficult,' Eric murmured.

'Damn right,' Stevens said and finished his wine. 'Look out there,' he said, gesturing past Marsdon Rock to where a tanker was outlined on the horizon, making its way south past Teesside. 'If that ship went down now, what a hell of a job finding her, recovering her! The sea is large and deep — and where fraudulent owners' vessels go down, usually inaccessible. An investigation can be a large waste of time and money. It's rare for an underwriter to get facts on which he can base a case; usually it's circumstantial allegations and inferences.'

'They won't go down too well in a court of law,' Eric murmured.

'That's been the Craig Lynch experience,' Stevens replied. 'And there's one other real beamer, directed straight at the underwriter's head.'

'What's that?'

'Barratry.'

'Ah.'

'You know about it?' asked Stevens.

'A wrongful act wilfully committed by master or crew to the prejudice of owner or charterer.'

'Absolutely right. But while you may know the definition, we bleed from the consequences. If a shipowner overvalues his vessel and then scuttles her to claim against a marine policy he doesn't *have* to rely on the perils of the seas clause. He can claim the bloody boat was wrongfully dealt with by the crew, to his prejudice. If he can actually show evidence that his ship was scuttled, that's all he has to do. Barratry is then *assumed* as far as the law is concerned.'

'And the underwriter has to pay up?'

'Exactly.'

'The underwriter could adduce evidence of the shipowner's involvement in the scuttling,' Eric suggested.

'How? By talking to the crew members? They wouldn't open their mouths — if you could find them. Sailors don't stay ashore long, and they don't take kindly to subpoenas to attend a hearing. They're inclined to take ship and disappear.'

'I see the problem,' Eric said.

'A few of many,' Tom Stevens sighed. 'But maybe they don't arise so often in Madrid.'

* * *

Back at his office Eric Ward checked his sources for a judicial view of the situation Tom Stevens had outlined to him. He found it in the 1923 case that Stevens had referred to: *General Shipping v. British General Insurance.*

. . . It must be borne in mind that underwriters who know their business very well and make large sums of money out of it for the most part favour overvaluation of hull and machinery. . .

It is no business of mine to tell underwriters how to conduct business which they do very successfully. I t suffices that they prefer overvaluation of hull and machinery . . .

* * *

The judge in that case, and in others Eric checked, had made no secret of his feelings. The judicial view was that little sympathy should be extended to underwriters: they brought fraudulent claims down upon their own heads by over-insuring ships against total loss.

At the end of the afternoon Eric walked up the hill to the offices of Stanley Investments. He took with him some photocopies of the judgements he had selected. Reuben Podmore was in his office. Eric handed the cuttings to him.

'We have a problem,' Eric said.

Podmore took from his top pocket a pair of pince-nez, adjusted them on his nose and read the cuttings quietly. Eric sat down while he read. At last Reuben Podmore solemnly removed his glasses, folded them, put them away and handed the cuttings back to Eric. 'Perhaps you can identify the problem for me, Mr Ward.'

'Stanley Investments is being saddled with an insurance claim which may well be fraudulent.'

'There's nothing in what you've shown me to suggest that is the case,' Podmore demurred.

'Overvaluation of hull and cargo is common enough, and as you'll see from the judgements in the past, it's a practice which underwriters even condone.'

'There's no evidence of such malpractice arising in the case of the *Sea Dawn*.'

'Because it hasn't been looked for, either by Storcaster or by Martin and Channing.'

'The issues arising from the loss of the ship have been dealt with both by an arbitrator and by the Commercial Court,' Podmore argued. 'I hardly think the matter of fraud would not have arisen—'

'It's possible the right questions were not asked,' Eric said doggedly.

'I see . . .' Podmore considered the matter for a little while. 'May I ask what you propose to do?'

'I think I'll have to meet representatives of Storcaster at Lombard Street, unless you have a meeting scheduled with them.'

'I have none. Instructions from Mr Channing were to the effect that the claims were to be processed, now that the legal issues have been settled.'

'Well, you stop the processing as of now.'

'Mr Channing won't like that.'

'To hell with Leonard Channing! These matters haven't been properly investigated, and if Channing thinks it's cheaper to pay up than investigate, all right, that's a point of view, but there's also the question of principle as far as I'm concerned. Something about the *Sea Dawn* claim smells; I'm not sure what it is, but I don't think we should simply pay out, even if there has been an arbitration and a court hearing. I'll not recommend payment until a few more questions have been asked — and answered. So, don't process the claims, and I'll fix up a meeting in London.'

'As you wish, Mr Ward.' Podmore stroked his jowls thoughtfully for a little while. 'You . . . er . . . you asked me to make certain inquiries about the Eurobond issue which was being arranged by the West German Deutsche Bank.'

'That's right. You have something?'

'I've got these papers which you might like to see.' He handed a folder across to Eric. 'The names at the bottom of the first sheet comprise a syndicate: a small group of co-managers have been invited to support the Deutsche Bank.'

'Martin and Channing are not among them,' Eric noted.

'They appear among the other list on the next sheet.' Reuben Podmore paused. 'In my view this isn't a very good time for Eurobonds. There was a good moment earlier in the month: a considerable number of companies decided it was time to borrow. The market's become choked with unsold securities and if you set that against the start of the year—'

'But Martin and Channing are supporting the issue.' Eric nodded and rose. 'I'll take these papers with me.'

Reuben Podmore rose also. He seemed hesitant and his eyes were doubtful as he looked at Eric. He laced his fingers together, rubbing his thumbs one against the other nervously. 'Mr Ward, may I say something?'

'Of course.'

'I . . . I wonder whether the actions you are contemplating are . . . wise.'

'Actions?'

'In the first instance, refusing to pay out on the *Sea Dawn* claim until you have pursued further inquiries. And secondly, contemplating a move into the Eurobond issues.' Eric looked at the investment manager calmly. 'Why do you think I'm not wise in these proposals?'

Podmore shrugged unhappily. 'The *Sea Dawn* affair, well, I'm not really qualified to comment. All I will say is that pursuing the issue is bound to raise hackles on Leonard Channing since he negotiated the business and has already advised the processing of the claim through Stanley Investments. I think he will be less than pleased at the development you propose. As for the Eurobond issue, I don't know what you can possibly be contemplating, but it hardly makes sense to enter that market through Stanley Investments when the parent company, Martin and Channing, are already involved.'

'Not even to get on the tombstone?' Eric asked.

'Mr Channing—'

'I don't really give a damn what Leonard Channing thinks about these issues,' Eric said evenly.

Reuben Podmore sighed. 'I think that really is the point that bothers me, Mr Ward. The wisdom of these tactics is doubtful as far as I'm concerned. The motivation, I suspect, only lends strength to my reservations.'

'My motivation?'

'Mr Ward, I don't wish to be impertinent. Nevertheless, I feel obliged to make the point. It seems to me you wish to pursue these actions out of a desire to obtain some form of satisfaction from Mr Channing. I think you feel he has bested you in some way, and you wish to get back at him. You may feel your actions will be justified; you may even feel there would be some justice in humbling Mr Channing by showing him he's wrong, or you can do better. But there's a remark I once came across: *revenge is a form of wild justice.* It's the wildness of it which I think must be called into question. I hope you take my meaning, Mr Ward.'

'I take your meaning, Mr Podmore.'

* * *

Eric Ward was left with the uneasy feeling that Reuben Podmore was right.

It was certainly true he was still smarting from the knowledge that Leonard Channing had outmanoeuvred him in the negotiations regarding Anne's investment in Martin and Channing. He felt that Channing had dismissed him almost contemptuously in giving him the opportunity to operate Stanley Investments: they both knew that Channing would still pull the strings from Lombard Street, and that Eric was still unable to have a voice in dictating policy in the parent company.

To that extent, Podmore had foundation for his suspicion that Eric might be trying to obtain revenge. Eric knew the full quotation too, from Bacon: *Revenge is a kind of wild justice which the more a man's nature runs to, the more ought law to weed it out.*

But as the train rushed him south of Darlington, on the main line to King's Cross, Eric tried to analyse his motives dispassionately and in doing so remained convinced that whatever Podmore might believe, as far as the *Sea Dawn* matter was concerned there was a principle at stake. And a sound business viewpoint to take.

Leonard Channing had underwritten the insurance cover for the Storcaster Syndicate. He had accepted the business and it had blown up in his face: Martin and Channing were accepting liability to pay out. But they wanted to do so through their subsidiary company in the North-East, and now that Eric had been given a say in the policy-making for Stanley Investments, it was only right that he should be given the opportunity to question the wisdom of merely paying out on the *Sea Dawn* claim without further argument.

On the Eurobond issue, well, maybe that was another matter. Eric was treading unfamiliar ground there, and would have to rely upon Podmore's advice and judgement. He would love to beard Leonard Channing in his own den, and there was a glimmering of an idea, which might possibly work, at the back of his mind. It would take nerve, and timing, and it would need Podmore's support — and it carried risks with it. He had tried to explain it to Anne.

Doubtfully she had said, 'The risks are high.'

'And the money is yours. If it didn't work, you'd stand to lose.'

'How much?'

'Who can tell?' he'd replied honestly. 'All I *can* say is that the returns on the other hand could be significant.'

'But so could the loss.'

'That's right.'

They had been sitting on the hillside above Elsdon, where they had ridden that morning. At their backs the rugged fells of Redesdale rose to the skyline, grey-green under the hazy morning sun. Below them they could see the eighteenth-century farmworkers' cottages scattered around the village green where cattle had been penned in the old days, against danger or severe weather. In the church, with its stubby spire, many of those who had fallen at the Battle of Otter burn had been buried in 1388, but Eric's mind had been on matters of more modern consequence as they sat there on their horses and looked down across Elsdon Burn flowing through its wooded ravine.

Anne had sighed at last. 'My father rated you, Eric, as a lawyer with a financial brain. As for me, well, I've always thought of you as a cautious man — look how long it took me to persuade you to marry me! But you don't undertake things lightly. You've been honest, and told me there's a risk of significant loss. But dammit, I've been trying to get you involved with my business affairs for a hell of a time, and it would be an odd thing now if I failed to take your advice.'

'I haven't offered any advice yet,' he had replied. 'You've outlined the possibilities — and the problems. I'm happy to let you take the decision in the end.' She straightened in the saddle and looked around her. 'After all, it wouldn't exactly leave us in a state of penury if we did lose out. We've still got this countryside to ride in, and Morcomb Estates capital is not affected by the deal.'

'You can trust me, Anne.'

'I've always known that,' she replied, and leaned across to kiss him.

Nevertheless, it was a responsibility he did not intend taking lightly, he decided, as the train thundered south. He had to be certain that the scheme half-formed in his mind was viable, and he had to be sure his judgement had not been clouded by his dislike for Leonard Channing and a desire to beat him at his own game.

* * *

Eric had made a hotel booking so he called there first, showered and changed. Leonard Channing had requested that they meet at six o'clock in the Lombard Street offices: thereafter, a private room at the Hilton had been arranged so that they could meet representatives of the Storcaster Syndicate over dinner that evening to discuss the claim in respect of the *Sea Dawn*.

The taxi deposited Eric at the offices of Martin and Channing precisely at five minutes before the hour. Eric entered the offices, took the lift upstairs and was met in the corridor by a woman with a supercilious air and chilly tone. Mr Channing had been delayed at a meeting at the Bank of England but expected to arrive within half an hour. Meanwhile, perhaps Mr Ward would care for some refreshment?

He had the feeling that his request for lime juice and soda both shook her and stretched the capacities of the refreshment cupboards at Martin and Channing. He also suspected that they would not be caught out twice: next time, they would even predict his choices.

The small ante-room between the secretary's office and Leonard Channing's personal suite was discreetly decorated in pastel shades and comfortably furnished. On the low table there was the usual annual report; the walls sported three *Spy* cartoons from the 1890s *Vanity Fair* magazine. Long-dead judges peered at him in caricatured form from their dark oak frames: their names were familiar to him as giants in their day, masters of sweeping judgements that had laid down principles and precedents that still held sway in modern times. In an odd way, they bolstered his resolve: there were established principles behind his stand against Leonard Channing.

The senior partner in Martin and Channing finally swept into his office at six forty-five. He did not come through the office in which Eric was waiting, but Eric heard the bang of the door beyond. There was a scurrying of secretaries:

Eric gained the impression that Channing was not in a good mood. Ten minutes later the lady with the supercilious air came into the ante-room and invited Eric to enter the presence.

Leonard Channing was standing near the window. The damask curtains moved heavily in the breeze that flowed in; Channing held a glass of whisky in his hand and his colour was a little high, as though he had yet to regain his temper after what must have been a stormy meeting at the Bank of England.

He swung around as Eric entered. 'Ward! They looked after you? Yes, I see they have. Sorry about the delay; got caught up. Bloody Treasury . . .' His eyes glittered angrily, and he sipped at his whisky. Then, abruptly, his eyes fixed on Eric. He gestured towards a chair and he himself sat down behind the ornate desk with the dark leather surface. 'Now then, what's all this nonsense?'

'Nonsense?' Eric queried calmly.

'When I got the call from Scholes I could hardly believe what he was telling me. Reuben Podmore had got in touch with him to say you were countermanding my instructions regarding the Storcaster contract, and that you were requesting a meeting with me. I think you need to get something clear, Ward. I'm the senior partner in Martin and Channing and the chief executive power within the firm. When I issue an instruction that a contract is to be honoured I damn well expect it to happen.'

'You said *honoured*, Channing.'

'I did. I entered that contract, it was on my judgement, and now we are liable under the contract we need to pay the claim. Any *delay* in the settlement reflects upon my word, my position in the company, and my authority as senior partner.'

'I would have thought your reputation would have suffered more if it can be shown it would be wrong to settle.'

'Wrong? What thc hell arc you talking about, man? The issues have already been before an arbitrator and the Commercial Court.'

'Some of the issues. Not all,' Eric replied calmly. Leonard Channing slammed the cut-glass whisky tumbler down on his desk. The golden liquid spilled, spreading over the leather, but he ignored it. A vein beat angrily in his forehead, and a faint line of perspiration was apparent on his upper lip. He was not used to being challenged, he had had a rough day at the Bank of England, and he clearly regarded Eric's attitude as an impertinence. But he was shrewd and was not prepared to allow anger to cloud his judgement. He paused, eyes glittering unpleasantly at Eric. 'I think we'd better get some things clear, Ward.'

'I agree.'

'I instructed Podmore to settle. You countermanded that. Whatever emerges in our discussions with Storcaster this evening I want it to be made clear: we'll be settling.'

'I can't accept that.'

'You've no bloody choice! You've no say in the policy-making or decision-taking of Martin and Channing and if I say we'll settle that's the end of it. Now, this evening, we can talk over the claim if you like, to save your face, and we can talk new business perhaps, or I'll simply treat the whole matter as one whereby I am *socializing* with the Storcaster people. But at the end of it we *settle*.'

'No. Not unless I'm satisfied.'

'*Satisfied*!' For a moment Eric thought Channing was going to rise and throw the half-empty whisky tumbler at his head. But the man controlled himself, lowered his voice threateningly. 'Your *satisfaction* doesn't enter into this, Ward. I don't think you know what you're getting yourself into here.'

'And I don't think you have thought the whole thing through clearly,' Eric replied.

Channing snorted. 'I'm denied clarity of thought, now! Fine, so tell me where I'm going wrong.'

Eric leaned forward in his chair. 'In the first instance, you say I can't countermand your order regarding the settlement of the *Sea Dawn* claim. The fact is you have no authority to insist I settle.'

'What the hell are you talking about?'

'You placed responsibility for the contract, and the settlement of the claim, with Stanley Investments. You have no official position with the company.'

'It's a subsidiary of Martin and Channing—'

'—and a limited company in its own rights. It has only one director — me — even though it depends for its financing upon Martin and Channing.'

Channing opened his mouth angrily to say something, then paused, thought better of it. He picked up his whisky tumbler and drained it. He set the glass down and stared at it for several seconds, then when he looked up his mouth was grim. 'The fledgling trying his wings, it seems. All right, Ward, the contract settlement was placed with Stanley Investments. A device merely, a way of dealing with tax—'

'But legal and effective, nevertheless.'

Channing did not like being interrupted. His eyes narrowed, and he snapped, 'That's easily remedied, then. I'll take back the responsibility for settlement. Martin and Channing can bear the brunt of a loss of this kind without too much of a tremor — and it's your own wife's investment that you're risking, after all. Hers, mine and others. Not yours, of course,' he sneered. 'But that's probably why you're adopting this ridiculous stance. So, let's settle it. I'll pull back the authority.'

'You can't do that.'

'Why the hell not?'

'Because you don't have the authority. You might regard yourself as the chief executive of Martin and Channing, and senior partner, but nevertheless decisions are taken by the board, even if they do follow your lead. The decision to place the settlement through Stanley Investments was a *board* decision and minuted as such. You have no authority to overrule that decision.'

'I'm chairman of the board. I could take chairman's action—'

'Not when a substantive motion has been taken, and your action is in direct contravention of that resolution. Besides, how would you find grounds to support your action? It was you who put the resolution to the board.'

Leonard Channing's anger was cooling. It was being replaced by something more deliberate and vindictive. He was not used to having his authority challenged, but he was not fool enough to bluster. 'I could call a special meeting of the board to withdraw the resolution,' he said quietly.

'Would you take that chance? And have a board member ask me what the hell was going on? When all I'd have to say would be that I was merely trying to protect the best interests of Martin and Channing and Stanley Investments — and their own money as board members and partners in the firm?'

Leonard Channing began to drum his fingers lightly on the leather top of his desk. His eyes were fixed on Eric's face but the glance was glazed as though Channing was seeing not the man in front of him but possibilities, ploys, the subterfuges practised through a lifetime of financial dealings in the City. The reflection calmed him, slowed his breathing, brought a cold passivity to his features and a dangerous quiescence which Eric knew could be a cloak for decision.

'I think,' Leonard Channing said stiffly, 'it's time we made our way to the London Hilton, to meet our friends from Storcaster.'

* * *

The dining-room was private, the table damasked, elegant cut-glass decanters glittered among the bottles and glasses and a discreet uniformed waiter dispensed pre-dinner drinks to the assembled group. There were four men in the room when Channing arrived with Eric: the manager who was organizing the room slipped away with the waiter once drinks had been served. Eric guessed he would return after an interval when the guests had settled down.

Saul Berckman came across and shook hands warmly with Eric. There was a welcoming smile on his lips and his dark eyes were friendly. He was dressed in a dark, well-cut suit and pale blue shirt that set off his swarthy complexion to advantage. 'You know Phil Daniels already, of course,' he said.

Eric nodded. 'We met in Channing's room.' Daniels bobbed his head, waved his dry martini in greeting but did not shake hands. His mouth was grim; there was an edge of hostility in his glance and Eric suspected that the three had been discussing the *Sea Dawn* policy before he and Channing had arrived, and whatever line the three men had decided to pursue it was not one with which Daniels was fully in accord.

Saul Berckman stepped aside, drawing Eric with him. 'Channing has already met Alain Germaine, but you won't have done so. May I introduce you to Alain — with me and Phil, he's a director of the Storcaster Syndicate.'

Germaine put down his brandy and soda to shake hands with Eric. He was small in build, but trim-waisted and with an air of confidence that was matched by his sharp, restless eyes. He was foxy-haired, its colour greying at the temples, and his grip was nervous and tense, as though he contained restless charges of energy he was eager to release. 'It's good to meet you, Ward,' he said in a slightly accented voice. 'I understand you're new to the business of risk underwriting. Welcome to the club.'

Eric was vaguely amused at the attempt to establish a platform: Germaine wanted to make it clear he regarded Eric's late attempt to hold back payment on the *Sea Dawn* account as the unwise action of a financial tyro.

Saul Berckman laughed. 'French clubs are unlike those in England. They are not necessarily used by gentlemen, and they can sometimes be less civilized. Competitiveness is not regarded as degrading.'

'I've never regarded myself as being particularly clubbable,' Eric replied.

The conversation generalized into a discussion of the English passion for clubs, which was not matched in Europe to the same extent. Berckman led the conversation with a practised ease, a *raconteur* who was used to establishing social relationships from which business contacts and contracts could be developed. Eric was not fooled by the easy image, however: the man was tough, and would be a good negotiator, not least because of his ability to dissemble. Very little remained unnoticed by Berckman: his glance was sharp, and he had a swift reaction time.

Phil Daniels was in a blunter mould. His personality matched his build: muscular, solid and direct, he would behave like a battering-ram at a conference and would require careful handling by his colleagues. Nevertheless, he would always be useful to them, for his directness would enable them to use him as a foil for compromise.

Alain Germaine was less predictable. The Frenchman was quick of mind and movement, but the tensions in him would not always be controlled. Eric gathered from the conversation that he had flown into London from Paris for this meeting, and would have received a briefing only hours before they were due at the Hilton. He seemed edgy, wishing to get back to his Paris office, and impatient that Daniels and Berckman could not have dealt themselves with the issues to be raised by Eric. Or maybe he felt that the issues should have been met head on by Channing, and not reached the stage of this conference.

Channing himself had remained slightly apart from the discussion. He stood with a whisky in his hand, but he was not drinking it. He was watching Eric, weighing up the situation, perhaps uncertain how far Eric would take his resistance in the face of the three Storcaster men. He had been quiet in the car that had brought them to the Hilton; he had been keeping counsel, in the face of Eric's forthrightness at his office. But Eric was not so naive as to believe he had overcome Channing: he had given the senior partner a few things to think about, but he had no doubt Channing would return at some point to the attack.

Phil Daniels downed his martini, walked across to the table and poured another for himself. He re-joined the group and suddenly interrupted the trivialities of the conversation. 'I gather you're the guy who's holding up the settlement of our claim, Ward.'

Eric looked at him, wondering whether this was to be a planned opening salvo. 'I represent Stanley Investments and—'

'And you don't go along with the outdated idea that an Englishman's word is his bond, hey?'

Eric smiled, refusing to react to the aggressive tone. 'I believe that when contracts are entered into they should be honoured.'

'But not if you're doing the paying out?'

'I don't object to payments being made in circumstances where they are due.'

'They're sure as hell due here!' Phil Daniels argued. 'So what's the reason for backing off?'

Slowly Eric said, 'I think it's a matter of interpretation. Your company clearly considers payment is due and should be made. There is another view—'

'Crap!' Daniels said bluntly.

Berckman stepped forward. 'Gentlemen . . .'

His intervention was a gentle warning that the waiters were arriving. The Storcaster group took their seats around the table, with Eric and Leonard Channing facing them. Eric noted wryly that Channing so seated himself that while he was beside. Eric he was also slightly distanced from him. It was a discreet reminder to all in the room that Eric Ward was holding an isolated position in these deliberations.

After the first course was served, it was Germaine who took up the matter. 'Phil, in his usual manner has come directly to the point. We certainly feel, as a group: somewhat dismayed at your attitude, explained to us by phone by Mr Channing.'

'Why dismayed?' Eric asked.

'All appropriate procedures have been followed,' Germaine said quickly. 'Arbitration . . . the Commercial Court . . . questions have been asked and answered—'

'But not perhaps the right questions,' Eric countered. There was a short silence. Phil Daniels began to say something but Saul Berckman raised a hand, interrupting him. 'Perhaps you'd care to elucidate for us,' he said to Eric. 'Clearly, since we have all been so close to the matter, there is the possibility that we have all missed something. You, as an *outsider*, may have spotted something we have not.'

'It's not quite that simple,' Eric suggested.

'Nevertheless,' Channing said, almost purring, 'I find myself in agreement with our friends. We do need to be specific if we are to hold up settlement.'

Eric paused. 'All right . . . but forgive me if I run over the salient facts of the *Sea Dawn* business, as I see them.' Berckman's glance was piercing. 'By all means,' he said. 'As I understand the position, the Storcaster Syndicate was approached by the owners of the *Sea Dawn* in respect of an insurance policy to cover hull and cargo.'

Alain Germaine raised his head. 'One moment . . . since you wish facts to be accurate, and since I negotiated the original deal after our agent, Cordóbes, in Spain got in touch with me, perhaps I should point out the matter was not an isolated one. The *Sea Dawn* insurance cover was one of a number of policies issued by us through a shipping company: Gaetano and Damant.'

'And because it was one of a number of policies, carrying risks involving quite large sums of money,' Phil Daniels added, 'we adopted our normal practice of laying off some of the risks through underwriting deals. It seems we made a mistake in asking Martin and Channing to underwrite, in that they have a leaning towards welshing.'

Leonard Channing said nothing and made no movement. Eric was on his own. 'The *Sea Dawn* was one of a number of policies,' Eric said, 'but the only one placed with us.'

'There were others placed with other underwriters,' Saul Berckman said. 'But you're not suggesting anything untoward in this, surely. It is common practice, as I'm sure Channing will confirm.'

'I can so confirm,' Channing said.

Eric glanced at the senior partner. Channing's eyes were on him, frosty and malignant. Whatever Eric might feel about the matter, he would get no help from Leonard Channing.

'I'll make no comment upon your choice of underwriter,' Eric said, 'or the number of policies you placed with Channing. Let's leave it at the moment that a hull and cargo insurance was taken out through your syndicate at competitive prices.'

Berckman hesitated. 'Competitive prices . . . yes, for the kind of business we were accepting.'

Eric eyed him calmly. 'High risk business?'

'You've read the transcript of the Commercial Court hearing, I imagine,' Berckman replied. 'High risk, yes, and so commercial rates also were . . . negotiated.'

'High rates.'

There was a short silence. Germaine broke in reluctantly. 'We found it necessary to place a high premium on the cargo. Machine tools—'

'And the hull?'

'The Commercial Court regarded it as a reasonable loading,' Daniels announced. 'What are you driving at, Ward?'

'Nothing yet. I'm merely establishing facts. Let's turn to what happened to the *Sea Dawn.* She left Marseilles with her cargo on the 25th of the month. A few days later, this 20,000-ton vessel radioed that she was in difficulties.'

'There was a problem, yes,' Daniels said. 'Engine trouble; a mechanical fault. It had no bearing on the issues here.'

'Apparently not,' Eric agreed, 'but according to evidence taken both at the arbitration and the Commercial Court hearing, it caused a certain delay. And the master took the opportunity to go ashore at Denia, on the Spanish mainland, during the delay.'

'He had negotiated the repairs with a Spanish firm. There were papers to be signed—'

'And maybe a woman to see,' Daniels interrupted angrily. 'So what? Where's this getting us?'

'It gets us to the point where the *Sea Dawn* foundered,' Eric replied. 'According to the evidence, the engines were repaired and the *Sea Dawn* continued on her way through the Mediterranean. But then, inexplicably, she sustained considerable damage below the waterline.'

'You use the word *inexplicably*,' Berckman said, 'but it is your word. It is not one the court used. A major hazard of all seagoing operations is the existence of submerged or semi-submerged debris. The court accepted that the *Sea Dawn* was damaged by one such hazard. We don't know, nor is it possible to find out, what the debris was, but it is clear from accounts given that the *Sea Dawn* struck some submerged wreck and sustained a hole below the waterline. It was not a serious problem and no request was made for assistance at the time.'

'But then, after an hour or so, they discovered that a fuel tank and the engine room were flooding.'

'That is so.'

'When did they discover that the engines of the *Sea Dawn* were liable to deteriorate rapidly?' Eric asked.

There was a short silence. Germaine glanced at Berckman, who was staring thoughtfully at Eric. It was Daniels who burst in again. 'It's obvious! If you get water in the engine room, you're bound to get a deteriorating situation.'

'I merely quote, verbatim, from evidence submitted,' Eric said mildly. 'The engines *were liable to deteriorate rapidly*. That was the statement made. My question is: when was that known? Only after the leak started? Or was it known before the voyage started? There is a certain ambiguity in the evidence.'

Quietly Berckman admitted, 'I will agree the ambiguity.'

'You made no inquiry into the state of the engines of the *Sea Dawn* before you accepted the policy from the owners?'

'It is not our practice,' Berckman said, still quietly.

Eric nodded. 'All right, let's go on. There was no great problem aboard the *Sea Dawn* at that stage. The damage could be handled. The water was pumped from the engine room, preventative measures were taken and they discovered that the hole below the waterline was about fifteen feet long. They would need a plate to cover the aperture left by the collision.'

'That is so,' Germaine agreed. 'But we know the facts. Are they in any way relevant to what we are here to talk about?'

'I think so,' Eric replied. 'May I go on? The protective plate had to be bolted to the hull. The method that had to be employed was that bolts had to be fired from a Cox bolt gun. There was one thing that puzzled me there. Is it common practice to have a skilled diver on board a ship, armed with such equipment?'

Saul Berckman's eyebrows were raised slightly. He shrugged. 'It may be a trifle unusual, but I would imagine it is not uncommon.'

'You imagine? You haven't checked?' After the silence developed around them, Eric went on, 'What *was* made clear at the hearing in the Commercial Court was that a Cox bolt gun has an explosive device which operates under water. But it can't be used, in circumstances such as applied in the case of the *Sea Dawn*, without elements of danger. The hole had been made near the engine room and a fuel tank. The fuel tank was the flashpoint, but the *Sea Dawn* master had caused the fuel to be pumped out. What he had *not* ensured, of course, was that the tank was free of gas.'

There was a discreet movement behind his left shoulder.

A waiter hovered, uncertain. None of the men had done anything more than barely touch their first courses. Negligently Channing waved his hand, instructing the waiter to clear the plates. 'Delay the next course,' he instructed. When the table had been cleared, Channing and the Storcaster representatives waited expectantly for Eric to continue.

'If other circumstances had prevailed, and the master of the *Sea Dawn* had called upon an independent contractor to come to his assistance, with an experienced diver, I wonder whether the situation would then have been different.' Eric speculated. 'The facts were, of course, there *was* a Cox bolt gun aboard, and there was also a diver prepared to use it. It wasn't clear from the court transcript whether the first mate, who was in charge directly of the operation, actually instructed the diver not to try bolting the plate until the tank was gas-free. All we do know is that he went down, started firing the bolts, and the result was an explosion which caused extensive damage.'

'It also killed the unfortunate diver,' Berckman commented.

'Which is why some crucial pieces of information were not available,' Eric added.

Phil Daniels leaned forward. 'Look, we're all familiar with the events leading to the sinking of the *Sea Dawn*. Why the hell you have to go over them again when what we want to know is why you're refusing to agree the settlement, I sure as dammit can't understand! Just what is needling you, Ward?'

'The explosion started a fire,' Eric said calmly. 'The master of the *Sea Dawn* radioed for assistance, but before additional help in fighting the fire could be obtained, and before a tow could arrive on the scene, the crew were forced to abandon and the *Sea Dawn* sank with full cargo. Salvage proved impossible and the claims began to come in.'

'And we dealt with them,' Berckman said. 'In the first instance, as we have submitted to Channing, we received the insurance claim and we raised doubts about it. We argued over the amounts involved, and under the terms of the policy the issue went to arbitration. The arbitrator took all facts into account: he commented upon the actions of the dead diver and found that the master had been negligent, through the first mate's allowing the Cox bolt gun to be used in such circumstances without first clearing the tank of gas. He also found that the damage was foreseeable. To that extent, he allowed a reduction of the amount payable to the shipowners. I take it you must agree we acted properly in these matters, Ward?'

Eric nodded. 'Of course. It was clearly necessary that you disputed the claim. The fact remains that the claim remained substantial in its award: three hundred thousand and more for the hull insurance and a separate two hundred and fifty thousand for the cargo.'

'That was the arbitration award,' Berckman pointed out, 'not our bid.' He paused. 'And we did not let the matter rest there.'

'Ah yes, there was the matter of the conduct of the master and the first mate.'

'Barratry. Our lawyers advised us we should clear the issue. It came before the Commercial Court. The judgement was that this was clearly a case of wrongful undertakings by the master, through his negligence, and the mate through his failure to issue appropriate instructions to the diver. The actions of the diver, as a member of the crew, also fell under the definition of barratry.'

'But the Commercial Court also held.' Germaine added, 'that this could not affect the award to the owners, since the act had been by the crew to the prejudice of the owners.'

'A decision in line with the precedents,' Eric agreed.

'So you agree we acted properly?' Daniels pressed.

'Of course.'

'Then what the hell's your argument against settling with us, as we've agreed to settle with the owners of the *Sea Dawn*?'

'As I said earlier,' Eric replied, 'though you might have raised questions with the arbitrator and in the court, perhaps they weren't the right questions. And maybe you asked your questions at the wrong time.'

'Goddammit, Ward,' Daniels snapped out, 'who the hell do you think you are? You walk into this business, raw as they come, and you suggest we're not alive to the problems of marine insurance, a business we've been building up for ten years and more? It's always easy to be wise after the event; of course we wouldn't have issued a policy on the *Sea Dawn* if we'd bloody well known she was going to founder, but the series of happenings was not predictable—'

'Wasn't it?' Eric interrupted.

Daniels blinked, glared at his colleagues and said, 'What the hell is that supposed to mean?'

'The arbitrator cut down the award considerably from the claim. But would the owners be quite satisfied with the award anyway?'

Berckman leaned forward.' They'd lost their ship—'

'Which perhaps was what they intended.'

Berckman smiled thinly. 'There's no evidence of that.'

'That's my point. How the hell do you know? You've never looked for such evidence, right from the beginning.'

The silence around him was hostile, Channing remaining watchful and observant while the three representatives of the Storcaster Syndicate bristled openly. 'You'd better explain that statement,' Daniels warned.

'The explanation is staring you in the face,' Eric said coldly. 'When you accepted the policy on the *Sea Dawn* did you check her out in the *Lloyd's Register of Shipping*?'

'Mr Ward—' Daniels began.

'Did you check on the transactions involving the *Sea Dawn* over recent years? How many times she was sold; what valuations were placed upon her by underwriters; whether there have been any surveys into her condition or seaworthiness by marine surveyors? When you entered the policy of marine insurance, did you check *any* of the details furnished you by the owners?'

'That's not the way the business operates,' Saul Berckman said, his eyes fixed on Eric.

'So I understand. But in my book it's not good enough. The fact is, if you didn't make such checks you should have. The questions should have been asked at the time you entered the policy; if you didn't, you were negligent.'

'It's an expensive business, my friend,' Alain Germaine intervened. 'The volume of business—'

'And no doubt the size of the premiums you demand,' Eric added.

There was a short silence. 'The fact is,' Saul Berckman said, 'business practice of the kind you seem, unrealistically, to criticize, does not invalidate our insurance cover with the shipowners. Nor does it invalidate the underwriting by Martin and Channing. After all, Leonard Channing asked no such questions either. Are you suggesting *he* was negligent?'

Eric looked at Channing. The senior partner in Martin and Channing looked relaxed, leaning back in his chair with his elbow on the arm, chin in the palm of his hand. But his eyes, fixed on Eric, held a mocking challenge.

'The wisdom of Channing's dealings with the Storcaster Syndicate is a matter that must be discussed within the firm itself, not with Storcaster representatives. And you are right: the contracts are not invalidated.'

'So,' Berckman said softly, 'there's no reason to hold up the settlement of the claim. You've had your say, we . . . ah . . . appreciate your point of view and the fact that your views are strongly held, but there's no reason now—'

'One moment,' Eric interrupted. 'Don't read too much into what I say. I haven't moved from my basic position. You didn't ask the right questions at the appropriate time. That doesn't mean we should ask no questions now.'

Channing sighed, as though they had reached a moment for which he had been waiting. Daniels glanced at Germaine in exasperation, but Saul Berckman remained watchful. He fingered the fading scar on his cheek thoughtfully. 'What are you driving at, Ward?'

'The arbitrator has decided upon the level of the award. The Commercial Court has adjudicated upon the matter of barratry. A wrongdoing did take place.'

'And it cannot affect the validity of the shipowners' claim under the marine insurance policy.'

'Unless they were party to the wrongdoing.'

Leonard Channing chuckled. It was a light, unpleasant sound. Eric did not turn his head. He stared at Saul Berckman. The man remained silent, holding Eric's gaze. Alain Germaine said, after a short pause, 'There's no evidence that the owners were involved in the events leading to the loss of the *Sea Dawn*.'

'How the hell do you know?' Eric snapped. 'You never asked the questions to try to find out.'

Germaine bridled. 'We've been trying to explain to you, Ward, that in the course of marine insurance there are certain things one has to accept. The volume of business, the fact that the assured is the only person who knows the true facts

. . . these are issues that are taken into account, and we load the premiums accordingly to cover contingencies—'

'That's right, but you don't know until after the event whether the vessel was overvalued, or the cargo insured more heavily than necessary, and if the ship goes down it's too damned expensive to find the evidence.'

'So what is it you propose to do, my friend?' Germaine asked angrily. 'What do you demand of us?'

For the first time, Channing intervened. He sat upright, raising his hand. 'I think, gentlemen, it is not possible for Ward to ask you to do anything. Rather, you should ask what *he* intends to do about it all.'

'I propose,' Eric said stiffly, 'to refuse a settlement until the answers to certain questions have been found.' Channing stared at him, a foxy smile touching his lips. 'It is not your expectation, surely, that our friends from Storcaster seek the answers?'

'They should have sought the answers before they agreed to settle with the owners. That should have preceded their claim against the underwriting contract with Stanley Investments.'

Channing's eyes glittered coldly. 'And if they find no evidence of involvement on the part of the owners, would you accept their statement? From what you've said so far, you seem to regard our friends here as lackadaisical in their attitude towards business.'

'I would certainly be interested to discover how seriously they had conducted the investigation,' Eric said.

'The hell with this!' Paul Daniels exploded. 'Just what is going on here? You're suggesting we don't know our own business, you're saying we should have carried out an investigation and you won't pay out till we do — and even then, if you don't like the results we come up with you'll be questioning our methods? Who the hell are you setting yourself up as, Ward? You trying to play God—'

'One moment.' Saul Berckman held up a warning hand.

His dark face was serious, his eyes fixed on Eric's face. 'I think we are likely to reach *impasse* unless we keep our tempers, and discover *exactly* what Mr Ward wants us to do. Only then will we be able to decide what action we take: the investigation he requests, or a painful, damaging and expensive suit—' he paused, glanced pointedly at Leonard Channing, and added—'against Martin and Channing.'

Leonard Channing elevated an eyebrow mockingly as he switched his own glance to Eric. 'We have the reputation and credibility of Martin and Channing on the line here, Ward. A suit, in which it is suggested we have welshed on an underwriting deal, will not stand us in good stead in the City. I think Mr Berckman's point is well taken. What precisely is it you will be requiring of them?'

Eric hesitated, as the Storcaster directors and Leonard Channing stared at him, waiting. 'There are a number of questions in my mind, and I think they require answers. I understand the business came to Storcaster through the agents Gaetano and Damant, but I don't recall being told who the owners of the *Sea Dawn* actually are.'

'Gaetano and Damant have been acting on their behalf—' Alain Germaine replied.

'I think we need to discover the identity of the claimants directly,' Eric insisted.

Saul Berckman's glance was cool.'

'All right, you want to know the identity of the owners. What else, Mr Ward?'

'I think we need to know what instructions were given to the crew with regard to the repairs carried out to the vessel, and what part was played by the first mate. Did he receive an order from the master, or was there an unauthorized order in respect of the use of the Cox bolt gun from the first mate to the seaman who died in the explosion?'

'Difficult,' Germaine murmured.

'We know, also, that the master went ashore at Denia. I think we need to know why he so acted, and what contacts he made there.'

'What the hell for?' Daniels expostulated. 'If his loins were itching, for God's sake—'

'We should be looking for possibilities of collusion between the owners and the crew on the issue of barratry,' Eric insisted. 'Tracing the movements of the master might produce evidence of such collusion.'

'Unlikely,' drawled Germaine. 'We should check,' Eric pressed.

'All right,' Saul Berckman said quietly. 'What more do you suggest we should be looking for?'

'Anything which points to the complicity of the owners of the *Sea Dawn* in its sinking. That includes the history of the vessel, its state and condition, the matter of whether it was over-insured or not . . .' He hesitated, then added, 'And perhaps we should look a little more closely at the events which may have followed the loss of the *Sea Dawn*.'

There was a short silence. When Eric said no more Phil Daniels shifted, awkwardly in his seat. 'Have I missed out on something here?'

Channing's gaze was vague; he was watching Eric but it was as though he had something else on his mind, his brain tracking over past occasions, sifting, trying to locate isolated incidents that might have relevance to their discussion. Alain Germaine leaned forward, smoothing his foxy hair in an unconsciously nervous gesture. 'What events, *specifically*, are you referring to?'

'The first mate on board the *Sea Dawn*,' Eric said slowly, 'was called Karl Mueller. He was the man who ordered the firing of the bolts into the plate, and caused the explosion that sent the *Sea Dawn* to the bottom.'

'So?' Saul Berckman questioned.

'Karl Mueller was recently fished out of the Tyne. Someone had slipped a knife between his ribs.'

'This is *bizarre*,' Leonard Channing said, almost in a whisper. 'Are you suggesting—'

'I think we should be looking, in addition, at the circumstances that might have led to the murder of Karl Mueller.'

The silence was complete as all four men stared at him as if he was crazy. Berckman was the first to recover. 'We're talking about a commercial contract, Ward, about what we see as an attempt by you to renege on an underwriting obligation. We're not concerned with criminal activity—'

'If the owners have been in collusion with the crew members of the *Sea Dawn*, yes, it's a commercial matter, but it can also amount to a criminal conspiracy. Where there's one crime, it can lead to another—'

'But there's no evidence of *any* bloody crime!' Phil Daniels almost shouted.

'Because you haven't looked for it,' Eric snapped.

'And you're seriously suggesting,' Leonard Channing intervened, 'that Storcaster should look into the possibility of a link between the murder of this man Mueller and the loss of the *Sea Dawn*?'

Before Eric could reply, Saul Berckman shook his head. His voice had hardened, an edge of steel creeping into his tone. 'That is impossible. This farce is going too far. I cannot see it is in any way incumbent upon us to follow this line at all. We have reached the impasse I feared. I am sure I speak for my colleagues when I say we cannot countenance any such burden being placed upon us. There is no alternative, I fear, to taking the necessary action to resolve this situation in a court of law.'

'Damn right,' Phil Daniels muttered angrily.

Alain Germaine was looking at his hands. There was a slight trembling of his fingers; it might have been nervousness, or it might have been anger. 'I am in agreement With Saul, Mr Channing. This thing is getting out of hand. Your . . . associate seems to me to have become . . . unbalanced in this matter. I also am of the opinion that if payment is not immediately agreed, there is no alternative but to sue.'

Leonard Channing's mouth was set like a trap. He glared at Eric, making no secret of his cold anger and dislike. 'I disagree, gentlemen. I am in complete sympathy with your views; I think this whole business is proceeding down avenues which are destructive both to the future of Storcaster and to that of Martin and Channing. But there *is* an alternative course.'

He glanced briefly at the three syndicate directors. 'I have no desire that my company should be joined in a damaging suit: mud sticks. To avoid such .a situation arising, all doors should be used. Mr Ward is unhappy about what has been done so far. He wants an investigation to be undertaken. So be it. But I am prepared to accept that the investigation should be no burden for Storcaster.'

Saul Berckman looked quickly at Ward and seemed to be about to say something. He subsided, as Channing continued.

'If Ward wants answers let *him* find them. If he wants to spend time on wild goose chases, it's *his* time. I can guarantee that the board of Martin and Channing will support my view that unreasonable demands are being placed on Storcaster. I propose, therefore, that since Ward is worried he should ask his own questions, and find his own answers.'

The silence was sharp, hostility almost crackling in the air. Leonard Channing smiled thinly, his eyes still cold and unpleasant. 'I don't propose to call a special meeting of the board, Ward. The next meeting is scheduled in three weeks' time. I would suggest you find the answers to your questions by that date. Otherwise, if you do not settle the claim of Storcaster for the underwriting of the *Sea Dawn* I shall be tabling a special resolution with the board. And I have no doubt that resolution will be approved.'

'What kind of resolution?' Eric asked.

Leonard Channing grunted dismissively. 'I shall propose an immediate settlement of the claim, following upon your resignation from· the directorship of Stanley Investments.'

'And if I fail to offer my resignation?'

'The board of Martin and Channing would divest you of that status by withdrawing its support of Stanley Investments, reconstituting the company or dissolving it. Your wife's investment would be secured in Martin and Channing, of course, but you, Mr Ward, would be *persona non grata* in every sense of the word as far as the business enterprises of Martin and Channing are concerned.' For several seconds Leonard

Channing allowed the hostility to shine out of his eyes as he glared at Eric. Then he sighed, in evident satisfaction that a problem had been resolved. Now, gentlemen, shall we dine?'

* * *

Eric Ward was forced to admit to himself that he had been somewhat shaken by the final turn of events. Once again he had made a miscalculation as far as Leonard Channing was concerned. At Lombard Street he had been confident that he had backed Channing into a corner from which the senior partner could not escape. In fact, Channing had already been planning the way out, even then: he had merely been waiting until Eric exposed his own hand in front of the Storcaster people — and he had ended up by manoeuvring Eric into a situation where all the problems were returned with interest.

As he returned northwards by train Eric considered gloomily that he had only himself to blame. Over-confidence had again cost him the battle with Leonard Channing, and now he had only a limited period of time within which to do the things he had been demanding of Storcaster.

He saw no reason to discuss the matters in detail with Anne. She asked for an account of the meeting with Leonard Channing and he told her of the Lombard Street conversation. When he came to tell her of the dinner with the Storcaster people, however, he was somewhat evasive. It was not that he feared appearing in a foolish light to her; rather, he was aware that if she knew in detail what he intended to do over the *Sea Dawn* affair she would become nervous, counsel caution, and perhaps try to stop him by insisting he should settle the matter at once by agreeing the underwritten payment.

He was less withdrawn with Reuben Podmore. He felt the investment manager had a certain right to know, because if Eric failed it was likely that changes would occur in the northern company. It seemed only fair to tell Podmore that it could end with the old man losing his job.

‘I appreciate your telling me, Mr Ward, and giving me an outline of the whole position.’ Podmore’s eyes were almost invisible behind his glasses as the light reflected from them, rendering them almost opaque. He and Eric were standing at the foot of Gray’s Monument during the lunch break. The meeting had been unarranged and casual, but Eric had thought it an appropriate time to discuss the matter.

Podmore turned his head and gloomily watched a group of children feeding some pouter pigeons as they strutted about the foot of the obelisk. ‘I have to say, nevertheless, that you have acted with a degree of circumspection, Mr Ward.’

‘You think we should settle the claim?’

Podmore pursed his lips and grimaced. ‘It’s not for me to comment upon your discussions with Mr Channing: you must determine for yourself how far you can carry — or rout — that gentleman. I’ve always considered him . . . formidable. But then, I’m merely an employee, an investment manager. Subservience colours one’s attitude and perceptions.’

‘And the Storcaster Syndicate?’

‘Again, a matter of judgement. There *is* a lot of money involved. It’s true they seem to have paid no great heed to the *possibilities* behind the loss of the *Sea Dawn*. But that, and the subsequent lack of investigation . . . well, it’s not uncommon in marine insurance, mainly because of the difficulties and costs of mounting such an investigation. And the bad publicity that might be engendered. All one can say, I suppose, is that you’ve given yourself a considerable task . . . and it was, perhaps . . . unnecessary to bring in the irrelevant issue.’

‘Irrelevant?’

‘The Mueller business.’

‘If it *is* irrelevant.’

‘Of course.’ Podmore sighed. ‘However, may I ask if there’s any way in which I can help?’

‘Do you want to?’

‘Whichever way one looks at it, Mr Ward, it is not in my interests that you should entirely lose your . . . ah . . . battles with Mr Channing. I stand to lose my job.’

'I'm grateful,' Eric said, and meant it. 'Well, clearly, I can use assistance and not least by way of advice.'

'Please ask.'

'I have some experience of criminal investigations, but mainly in the North-East, and in matters of minor importance. I imagine that where the shipping world is concerned there are reliable firms who will carry out confidential investigations of a specialist kind.'

'Specialist work carries specialist fees, Mr Ward,' Podmore warned.

'I'm aware of that. But in the first instance I want as much background as I can possibly raise on the *Sea Dawn* by way of her history and condition.'

'It will mean checking on her registrations, the flags she'll have sailed under, and a trace of her ownership history. I take it you'll also want any survey results, and commercial contracts, charter — parties and the like, that she might have been committed to.'

'Anything that may be relevant.'

'It will be expensive.'

'I expect so.'

A five-year-old child broke away from its mother at the top of the Tynerider station and ran forward, scattering the pigeons. They rose with a flurry of wings, circling the monument in a grey and white cloud. Podmore observed them dispassionately. 'I think I can put you in touch with a London firm,' he said slowly. 'They specialize in marine investigations. They have the advantage of being able to pick up supposition as well as fact. You may well find there is more of the one than the other. The shipping world . . . it is a curious one. And it is awash with rumour.'

'Sea-salt gossip.'

Podmore shrugged. 'Is there anything else, Mr Ward?'

'Mueller.'

Podmore observed him gravely. 'Are you sure it's wise to pursue that issue.'

'Why?'

'It can muddy waters more than is necessary. It can give rise to obsessions; make innocent situations appear sinister. It's a police matter, and unlikely to have any connection with the *Sea Dawn.* Seamen often live dangerous and complicated lives.'

'It needs checking out,' Eric insisted stubbornly.

'So you wish Mr Mueller's movements also to be traced?'

'If possible.'

Podmore sighed. 'All right, I will see what I can do. I should return to the office now, I'm afraid.'

'I'll walk with you. It's on my way to the Quayside.' They began to walk the short distance down Gray Street to the corner where Podmore would be turning off to go back to his office. The street dipped gracefully away before them, the colonnaded front of the Royal Theatre standing resplendent after its cleaning. At the corner, Eric paused, and Podmore looked at him expectantly.

'The Deutsche Bank issue,' Eric said.

A wary frown appeared on Podmore's brow. 'I had hoped we would have no further necessity to discuss that, Mr Ward.'

'What's the present situation?'

Podmore hesitated, then shrugged reluctantly. 'I did suggest it was a bad time for the issue with the market choked. I mean big borrowers like Texaco, the Swedish Government, Sears Roebuck and Allied Lyons have been in the market.'

'And?'

'My information is that a number of investment banks have been trying to get mandates for the issue.'

'Which ones?'

'In the main, the dominant American and Japanese firms who have branches in London.'

'What's been the Martin and Channing position?' Podmore glanced around him and wrinkled his nose as though he found it indiscreet and tasteless to discuss such confidential business on a street corner in Newcastle. 'They're holding on to their mandate and not allowing their underwriting share to be split. They don't want to risk their position on the tombstone.'

'Even if it costs them money in the long run?'

Podmore looked at him uneasily. 'I have no say in policy, Mr Ward.'

Eric thought for a moment, staring blankly at Podmore, as the blood began to quicken in his veins. 'So Martin and Channing are staying pat. What about the other firms?'

Podmore shifted his weight from one foot to another, like an elderly schoolboy afraid of being caught in a misdemeanour. 'I . . . I did stress that in my view there's been a miscalculation in the timing of the issue. Other firms have been facing up to the facts.'

'*What facts*?'

Podmore sighed unhappily. 'The tombstone leaders are, in the main, large firms. Martin and Channing is one of the smallest and it's keen to retain its position on the tombstone. The other firms have . . . higher reserves and sounder financial positions. They have less to lose . . .'

'So they're spreading the risk,' Eric murmured.

Podmore nodded. 'Their calculation will be that as long as they remain on the tombstone it doesn't matter too much if they divest their commitment considerably.'

'Whereas Leonard Channing wants to retain a larger credibility for his firm than it perhaps deserves . . . What level did they come in on at the issue?'

'Mr Ward . . .'

'What was the percentage, Podmore?'

The investment manager hesitated unhappily. 'I . . . I believe it was nine and seven-eighths.'

'And what's happening now?'

Again Reuben Podmore shifted his bulk nervously. 'You must understand the situation, Mr Ward. Bad timing like this, it brings out the worst in people. The sharks gather. They see the potential in the situation and they take advantage of it. The major underwriters — the ones who came together in the first instance — they will have had to come in at nine and seven-eighths in order to make the issue viable. But some of them will now be facing the reality of the market place.'

'They'll be releasing bonds with a lower interest rate, to other underwriters.'

'I'm afraid so.' Reuben Podmore blinked rapidly, staring at Eric Ward. 'There's a large part of the City which will have stayed away from the issue, unable to get in on the syndicate. It will be below them to tout for the business thereafter — even to get on the tombstone — particularly if the interest is shaved to an unrealistic figure.'

'And it is being shaved that way?'

'Yes. They'll be wringing their hands, Mr Ward, speaking of the good old days when you could trust your friends, and railing at what they see as the insanity of those entrepreneurs who will now be winning business by offering the issue at unrealistic interest rates.'

'And those managers will, of course, be hoping that the short term interest rate will fall.'

'Making the low interest bonds attractive, yes, Mr Ward.'

'That situation would be a problem for Martin and Channing, wouldn't it?'

'It *is* a problem.'

'Then I think, Mr Podmore, we should be taking a hand in the game.'

* * *

Reuben Podmore's eyes had almost started out of his head. For a few moments he had thought Eric was joking; then he had turned a bright red, and finally he had insisted that Eric come along to his office. He had hurried up the stairs, curtly suggested to his secretary that she go out and do some shopping, and then in the privacy of his office he had sat down, wiped his brow and demanded that Eric reconsider the suggestion.

'I have to say, Mr Ward, that what you suggest is unsound financially, and certainly unethical.'

'Why is it unsound?' Eric asked.

'If Stanley Investments attempt to win business by issuing the Eurobonds at an interest rate shaved below the realistic figure it would be an unsound risk to take. Any significant movement in the interest rates could cost the company thousands of pounds—'

'If the rates move the wrong way,' Eric countered. 'But that is a possibility!'

'Yet you've already told me that the Deutsche Bank issue has arisen at a bad time. The syndicate managers including Leonard Channing — have agreed to underwrite the issue at nine and seven-eighths per cent. If the bond issue sticks, with sales and movement becoming possible only at the lower rates, it's Martin and Channing who'll be taking the big risk.'

'That's true, Mr Ward, but they can afford it.'

'Afford to lose large sums of money that way? On a bad business risk, just for the pleasure of getting their names on a tombstone — a tombstone that might later get the reputation of really having buried a few reputations?'

'If the issue is really bad business in the end it won't be trumpeted, Mr Ward. You just don't understand—'

'I understand enough to know that if we take up issue rights at a lower interest rate — and succeed in selling the bonds thereafter at a better rate than we paid for them it will be good business for Stanley Investments.'

Podmore sweated. 'That's true, but it would require delicacy of touch, a buying in of the rights at the appropriate time, a gamble that the interest rates will move in the right direction—'

'But that's always the risk that's being taken.'

'All right, Mr Ward,' Podmore snapped nervously, 'but what about the ethics of the situation?'

'That,' Eric said coolly, 'you'll have to explain to me.' Podmore fiddled nervously with the papers on his desk as he tried to find the right words. 'Stanley Investments is a subsidiary of Martin and Channing.'

'But an investment company in its own right, with its own management.'

'Quite so, Mr Ward, but a subsidiary, nevertheless. Its policy is dictated by the main board—'

'Not so, Podmore. It has had no policy, to date. It has merely accepted business for Martin and Channing, fronted for its losses for prestige and tax purposes, and has indulged in little or no trading activity on its own account.'

'That only emphasizes its dependence, surely—'.

'But things have now changed with the Martin and Channing board decision to establish me as a director. That enables me to undertake policy decisions for Stanley Investments — *independently of Lombard Street!*'

Podmore stared owlishly at Eric. Now that he could see the glint of determination in Eric's eyes he was becoming calmer, more rational in his opposition, and less nervous. He put away his handkerchief and laid his hands flatly on the table in front of him. 'It is completely illogical that you should act as sole director in this situation, Mr Ward.'

'But not illegal, Podmore. Under the Companies Act the minimum number of directors in a private company is one. In a public company, two. My wife has already intimated she would accept a directorship and work with me, if necessary. There's no problem.'

'It is still wrong ethically,' Podmore said portentously. 'Martin and Channing have taken up the bond issue at nine and seven-eighths. If you obtain a mandate at a lower rate, and issue and sell, you would be undercutting them. They might be forced to hold on to the issue, at considerable loss to the company, over a period of weeks, maybe months.'

'With the number of bonds we bought, we could hardly be blamed for that.'

'True,' Podmore admitted, 'but you would nevertheless be *one* of the traders who would be undermining their position. That would be seen as unethical by the Martin and Channing board—'

'But fun, Podmore,' Eric said, grinning, 'if we made it.' For a moment he caught an answering flicker on Podmore's lips, and then the investment manager's caution came back. He shook his head. 'I must counsel against it, Mr Ward, seriously. The financial risk is great. The ethics are not insignificant — the impact upon your tenure here and upon the board of Martin and Channing would be severe. I really must advise you against this step. Not least because there is the additional problem of persuading anyone to give us a mandate, with our track record.'

'As a subsidiary of Martin and Channing?'

'Mr Ward, I was afraid you were going to say that,' Podmore replied mournfully. 'I beg you . . . please think it over.'

Eric had promised to do so.

Now, five days later, as he sat once more in Podmore's office, he had still not made up his mind.

He had to admit there was force in Podmore's argument.

He had talked it over with Anne, over dinner at Sedleigh Hall. 'You see, if Reuben Podmore tries to obtain a mandate to place these Eurobonds he'll have to show the sellers that he has the reputation and financial credibility of Martin and Channing behind him. They may well think it odd that Stanley Investments will be undercutting Martin and Channing but they won't ask too many questions: they'll consider it as a back-up arrangement whereby Martin and Channing are trying to protect itself for some of the issue.'

'A sort of laying off of bets by bookmakers who get too much money placed on a particular horse,' Anne murmured.

'Something like that. The trouble is, Martin and Channing won't know about it, and Stanley's investment in the Eurobonds at a lower rate of interest could be seen as an attack upon the profitability levels Martin and Channing are hoping for.'

Anne shook her head. 'The amounts of money you're talking of won't buy enough of the issue to seriously affect Leonard Channing's profitability hopes.'

'Not standing alone, of course,' Eric agreed. 'But there are a number of sharks feeding off the main placement; taken together, their actions could be seen as damaging to Channing.'

'But it's not illegal?'

Eric shook his head. 'No. In Podmore's view it could be construed as disloyalty and sharp practice but it's certainly not illegal, in view of the independence of the Stanley Investments board as it is newly constituted.'

Anne sipped, her wine, thoughtfully weighing up the situation. You've described these investment managers you'd be joining as sharks.'

'It's how Leonard Channing would describe them.' Anne snorted. 'He's no placid sea trout waiting to be gobbled up himself! He's a predator, if ever I saw one. So why should you worry about his opinions of your conduct?'

But maybe that was one of the problems facing Eric: the basic motivation for his proposed action could well be merely the urge to beat the merchant banker at his own game. He was still smarting from the knowledge that he had been outmanoeuvred by Channing: if he was not careful the feeling could become obsessional — and obsessions clouded judgement.

* * *

For that reason he remained undecided as he sat in Reuben Podmore's office facing the young man the investment manager had introduced as James Olsen, from the investigative agency in London. Olsen had brought an interim report with him; he held it in his hands, for reference.

'All right,' Eric said, 'what have you got? Perhaps we could start with the matter of the *Sea Dawn* herself.'

Olsen nodded, shifting easily in his chair. He was about thirty years of age, with the clear, distant look and .tanned skin of a man who knew the sea. He was slightly built and casually dressed but there was a whipcord leanness about his upper body that suggested he was fit, active and more than able to look after himself in a tight corner. The livid scar above his right eyebrow suggested he had found himself in more than one such corner already. He had an easy smile and a pleasant manner, no doubt useful attributes when he was asking questions, but behind the eyes there was a shadow of tension an almost involuntary muscular response to an environment that held elements of perpetual hostility.

James Olsen did not trust the world, and to that extent was a cynic.

'Okay, the *Sea Dawn*,' he said. 'We've managed to turn up a fair bit of information about the old girl, including her owners, her charter-parties and her contracts, since the time she was built thirty years ago.'

'Thirty years!'

James Olsen smiled thinly. 'Dusseldorf-owned. First registration 1954.'

Eric glanced at Podmore but the investment manager was staring thoughtfully at his clasped hands. Maybe he was seeking solace in prayer.

'I've not been able to trace much of her history during the first ten years although I would guess she was used for various charter-parties in Northern Europe. However, there's a new registration in 1965: she was bought by the Fina Italia Company, and was operated along the West African and Ivory Coast routes. As far as I can make out, ownership was transferred around about 1973 to Gibbs International.'

'A new base?' Eric asked.

'A South African company, so the *Sea Dawn* was used out of Durban on voyages to Europe via the Cape.'

'She seems to have got around.'

'You could say that,' Olsen agreed drily. 'In 1978 there was a bill of sale registered in favour of Oakbrook and Brightman; thereafter, the *Sea Dawn* made regular trips around Dakar and Senegal.'

'What was the sale price at that time?' Reuben Podmore asked quietly, raising his eyes from his hands.

'Around forty thousand pounds.'

Eric caught the steady glance Olsen gave him. The investigator seemed to expect Eric to make some comment, but when none was forthcoming he smiled slightly and went on.

'The present owners would seem to be a firm called Brandon Roskill, incorporated in Madrid in 1983. They purchased the *Sea Dawn* at around about that time, and since then she's been used for charter-parties in Italy, Spain and France. Contracts have often been negotiated with Gaetano and Damant, the Paris shipping merchants. The vessel has been used largely for the transport of mechanical parts, engines, machinery of various kinds.'

Eric nodded thoughtfully. 'I see. Tell me, have there been any condition reports?'

James Olsen hesitated, glancing at his papers. 'They're notable by their absence, by and large. There was a survey made for insurance purposes in 1967, but it's too old to be of much use to you, I would guess. It was OK. More to the point, perhaps . . .'

'Yes?'

'Shortly before the *Sea Dawn* was sold by Fina Italia to Gibbs International she was the subject of an insurance claim.'

'Of what kind?'

'She was involved in a collision with another ship. A tug was brought alongside and a standard Lloyd's form of "no cure — no pay" salvage agreement was signed. She only just managed to stagger into port under tow, and there was a bit of a battle over the insurance claim. It was finally settled out of court.'

'For how much?'

'Not divulged. The *claim* was large, but I suspect the claimants backed off and accepted a lower sum in the end rather than have too many questions asked.'

'I see . . .' Eric thought for a moment. 'There's been nothing by way of condition reports since then?'

'Not that I've been able to trace. But you must remember, they'd only arise really where insurance cover was getting awkward. On the other hand . . .'

Eric looked at the investigator. Olsen eyed him almost mockingly, as though testing him. 'Well?'

'It depends, Mr Ward, whether you want facts only, or whether you want suppositions, too.'

'Tell me.'

'These aren't facts, just gossip. The waterfronts suggest the *Sea Dawn* was a rust bucket.'

'What's that mean?'

'She was seaworthy, but only just, and ripe for a retirement out of which the owners could obtain maximum financial advantage.'

'By over-insurance?'

Olsen shrugged. 'There are ways.'

Eric considered the matter for a short while. 'All right,' he said at last, 'if the *Sea Dawn* was a rust bucket, as you suggest, what price would the owners be likely to get, if she had been broken up for scrap?'

Olsen pursed his lips. 'Difficult to say, but probably about twenty to thirty thousand quid.'

Eric stared at him. 'She was insured for more than ten times that amount.'

Olsen grinned. 'Maybe they'd repainted her.' He shrugged, the smile fading. 'You have to remember, Mr Ward, there's always going to be an *element* of over-insurance. I mean, it's not just the scrap value of the ship that has to be covered. There's also the price of replacement to be considered, and underwriters will normally make some allowance for that, although they'll also adjust the premium, naturally. But they know what's going on.'

'To the extent of ten times the amount, over-insuring?' Olsen shook his head vaguely. 'That does seem a bit . . . excessive, sure. But there might have been special circumstances.'

'Such as?'

Olsen's eyes were blank. 'Not for me to say.'

Eric waited but the man was not forthcoming. 'Anything else?'

'She was held for a bill of lading difficulty at Mena al Ahmadi in the 'seventies, and a price was placed upon her then. I've not been able to get it yet, but I could keep chasing—'

'No, I don't think that'll be necessary,' Eric interrupted. 'I think I've got enough to work on . . . Now then, did you find out anything about Karl Mueller?'

Olsen's eyes were vague. 'Not strictly my line of business, Mr Ward. And seamen move around. I take it you didn't want any kind of potted history of his career?'

'No, just his movements since the loss of the *Sea Dawn*.'

Olsen shrugged. 'Little to tell, then. He was present at the arbitration, and put in an appearance as a witness at the court hearing. But he had no berths during that period — which could be the result of the *Sea Dawn* sinking, of course.'

'That's a fairly long period without work.'

'Maybe he had savings behind him,' Olsen said flatly. 'So he'd not been in work until he joined the *Gloria* as master?'

'It would seem so, though I can't be certain, naturally. He picked her up at Marseilles, when the skipper went sick. There are rumours about the situation—'

'I've heard them,' Eric said grimly.

'Seems a bit bizarre, just to get a berth.'

'Unless he had a reason for coming to Tyneside, or England.'

'There are such things as jets,' Olsen countered. 'And there is an airport at Newcastle.'

Eric let it pass. 'Is there anything else?'

James Olsen hesitated. He toyed with the papers in front of him, as though uncertain how to proceed. 'I deal in facts, not rumour, not least because seamen can spin the largest tales . . . On the other hand, I did pick up something which is being remarked upon since Mueller's death was reported.'

'What's that?'

'The suggestion that the *Sea Dawn* was bad news, jinxed, an albatross boat.'

'How do you mean?'

'At Mena al Ahmadi, in the 'seventies, two of the crew died, one of hepatitis, one of cholera. In 1977 the first mate had a heart attack in Durban.'

'That's all rather a long time ago,' Eric said slowly, watching Olsen.

'Mmmm.' Olsen shrugged. 'On the other hand, Mueller isn't the first guy to die since the sinking of the *Sea Dawn*: there's been another death among the crew.'

'When?'

'Preceded Mueller by about six weeks. He was a Glaswegian, called Fred Trainor. Killed in a car crash, outside Paris.'

'Trainor . . .' Eric paused. 'He was one of the crew?' Olsen busied himself with his papers. 'He was the master of the *Sea Dawn*, actually.'

The man who had gone ashore when the engines failed at Denia.

* * *

It was a thought that remained buzzing in the back of his mind during the next two days. He did not discuss it with Anne, but he knew that he would have to do something about it, and on the Thursday he arranged a booking on the Newcastle-Alicante flight at midday.

At nine that morning he called in to see Reuben Podmore. 'I've decided I'll have to go to Spain, to check out what I can regarding this man Trainor's stopover at Denia.'

'What is there to discover, Mr Ward?'

'I don't know. The Storcaster people mentioned that he had certainly called to see their agent in Javea, Cordóbes. Maybe I can start there.'

'It seems a wild goose chase to me,' Podmore averred boldly. 'In the end, even if this was a rust bucket fraud, I don't see how you're going to be able to prove it.'

'I've got to try,' Eric said. 'Anyway, I'll be away for a few days. While I am away, I want you to do something for me.'

Alarm registered in Reuben Podmore's eyes. 'I hope you're not going to—'

'I've thought it all over,' Eric interrupted him calmly. 'I'm not persuaded by your ethical arguments; the power of decision lies with Stanley Investments. So I want you to make the necessary contacts. And I want you to wait, watch the interest rates.'

'Mr Ward—'

'When you think you can take up issues at a rate of nine and a half I want you to buy in.' He handed Podmore a letter. 'I've written your instructions there, with the amount of cover so there's no misunderstanding. The letter will also absolve you from any repercussions if things go wrong.'

'Mr Ward, they *will* go wrong,' Podmore said mournfully. 'You don't understand. The market rate trends are not good. A shift in the wrong direction—'

'And I'm out in the cold,' Eric said grimly. 'I know that. But the decision's been made. Follow it through.'

He knew the risk he was taking. He knew that financially he would not be hurt, in a personal sense, since Anne was backing him. But he was aware that failure .could bri.ng Stanley Investments crashing down around his ears, with his credibility, even with Anne, seriously impaired. Yet a streak of stubborn independence forced him on, even against the advice and wise counsel of Reuben Podmore.

And deep inside his own head, there was also the small voice that told him he was being unwise, obsessed by the desire to balance the books in his personal battle with Leonard Channing.

* * *

On the flight he tried to sleep.

Eric did not like flying. There was the memory of a flight to London, shortly after he had undergone his iridectomy, a memory that could still bring the sweat out on his forehead at night when he lay in the darkness, recollecting the shuddering, lancing pain he had suffered behind his eyes. As a result he rarely flew, taking the train when he needed to travel to London. He had not been looking forward to the flight to Alicante.

On take-off he had felt a prickling behind his eyelids but it was probably psychosomatic in origin. He felt no real pain or discomfort. But he did not sleep, either . . . he was unable to stop his mind churning over the decision he had taken with regard to the Eurobond issue, doubting its wisdom, weighing up the chances of a successful raid into the market against the probability of the disaster that Podmore predicted. Threading through those anxieties was the skein of doubts he also felt about his challenge to the *Sea Dawn* underwriting. In so many ways Eric was laying his reputation and his own self-esteem, upon the line, and in a business with which he was largely unfamiliar. Olsen had given him little to go on and yet here he was, flying to Spain to discover he knew not what, and he had no real idea what might lie at the end of his inquiries.

At best, perhaps, he would discover further questions to put to the Storcaster Syndicate and Leonard Channing. At worst, the result would be humiliation and a resignation from Stanley Investments.

The anxieties were still niggling at him when the plane touched down at Alicante and he emerged on to the burning tarmac of the airport. There was little delay at immigration, baggage collection and Customs. He had made arrangements at Newcastle for a hire car to be available at the airport: it would be a two-hour drive on the motorway north along the Costa Blanca to Denia. At the exit barrier he found himself surrounded by a jostling throng of tourists. He pushed his way through, trying to identify the representative of the car hire company.

He was totally unprepared for the booming, chuckling voice that came from behind him as he pressed forward.

'Ward! I was beginning to think you'd never get here! Welcome to Alicante!'

Eric turned. He stared, speechless.

Standing with his hands spread wide, beaming a welcome, was Halliday Arthur Lansley.

CHAPTER 4

When the sun dropped below the ragged outline of the mountains inland, the moon lifted and the sky shaded in red and gold, fading through tones of rose to a pale lavender. As the moon climbed it brightened, transmuting the sea into molten silver, the spray glittering as it blew aft, bright against the dark land mass of the Costa Blanca. The lights of the harbour at Alicante, picking out gleaming yachts and work-scarred fishing-boats, had long since faded behind them, and the white beaches and rocky cliffs northwards were blurred into darkness. The breeze was warm on Eric Ward's face and the sound of the rushing water beneath the bows susurrated soothingly in his ears. He stood on the deck, holding the rail and he smelt the salt wind, tangy and sharp.

'*La Encantada*. The Enchanted One. On an evening like this, all is enchantment, is it not?'

She was tall and slim, her dark hair straight, shoulder-length, curling softly at the nape of her neck. She wore a sheath dress, virginal white, deep-shadowed where it was cut to the curve of her breast. Her eyes were violet in colour, he had noticed, deep in their intensity, and she moved with a feline grace, a long swing of the hip that demonstrated agility, litheness and an overt sexuality that would fire any man. She was called Elaine, and she was perhaps twenty years of age.

Halliday Arthur Lansley hadn't changed, Eric thought. He recalled his first meeting with the man. It had been on board the *Alouette*, in the harbour at La Canebiere. On the after-cockpit of the white, shark-like craft, Lansley had been waiting, sixty years old, sixteen stone in weight, and no more than five feet three tall. There had been three girls on board on that occasion: Catherine, Villette and Jeanne-Marie. They had been blonde and lissom, unostentatious and available. They had caused Eric a sleepless night. Lansley had caused him more than that.

He had heard of the man before he had met him. Lansley had been a property developer in the North-East when there was money to be made, quickly, and on the edges of legitimacy. When the corruption scandals had broken he had not emerged cleanly: indicted on several charges of fraud and corruption, he had been sent to prison but had not served the full term. By a judicious movement of funds and holdings he had managed to avoid the loss of all his ill-gotten gains, and a deal with the authorities together with heart trouble, had led to his early release.'

It was his involvement with Morcomb Estates and a land charge in El Centro that had caused his path to cross Eric's, but thereafter they had found their interests coinciding not entirely to Eric's benefit.

The man was an incorrigible rogue. His last words to Eric had been that he hoped they would meet again. Eric had replied he hoped otherwise. And yet here he was once more in Lansley's company and aboard one of Lansley's playthings, the motor yacht *La Encantada*.

With another of Lansley's playthings, Elaine, standing close beside him.

The girl touched his arm gently. 'It's a beautiful night, a time for enjoying the deck. But Mr Lansley has finished his work now, and dinner is available. He requests that you join him.'

Her voice was soft, her accent French, and her smile inviting. She moved ahead of him, as aware as he of the movement of her body. He stooped to enter the dining-room: Lansley was standing by the table, a dry martini in his hand.

'Ward! As I recall, you don't drink. But a little wine to celebrate the occasion?'

'A little wine, perhaps. But not to celebrate.'

'You're not enamoured of meeting me again!' Lansley laughed in high good humour, his flabby cheeks wobbling, his Pickwickian contentedness as self-satisfied as Eric remembered. 'That's what I've always liked about you, Ward. Honesty and directness. Admirable qualities. You've not changed since last we met.'

'Nor have you.'

Lansley's lightweight suit was well tailored and expensive its styling disguising the bagginess of his body, the sagging paunch and the flabbiness that high living had brought back to him since the searing experience of imprisonment.

He had put on more weight since Eric had seen him last, and his hair had thinned even further, emphasizing the blotchiness of the skin of his forehead. He stood facing Eric, rocking lightly on his feet, waving his wineglass negligently as Eric was handed a glass by the quiet, too well-muscled waiter in the white shirt and slacks, more guard than waiter.

'I'm glad we were able to meet at the airport. Such a boring drive, the motorway north to Ondara. By sea, now, it is much more pleasant, refreshing. Our meeting was a happy chance.'

'I always have the feeling chance plays little part in your life, Lansley.'

Lansley chuckled. He eyed the girl called Elaine as she moved smoothly towards him with a glass of cool white wine. 'I must admit I make what plans I can. At my age, and in my state of health, one must leave as little as possible to chance.'

'So how did you know I was coming to Alicante?' Eric demanded.

Lansley raised his eyebrows in mock surprise. 'Surely, dear boy, you must know now that I have so *many* friends in the North-East, and that I like to have all the gossip, learn what's going on in my enforced absence.'

'What interest can you possibly have in my business?' Eric asked bluntly.

Lansley slipped his arm around the girl and caressed her, almost absent-mindedly, as his sharp little eyes fixed their glance on the rim of his wineglass. 'Come now, you know I have almost a . . . fatherly interest in your affairs. I like you, Ward, I like your style, your independence and your occasional bloody-mindedness. You were helpful to me a little while back, and when I heard you were flying to Spain it seemed the least I could do, meeting you, giving you transport to Javea, entertaining you—'

'I'm not simple-minded, Lansley.'

'No.' The eyes moved, the glance on Eric sharp and piercing. Lansley chuckled and shook his head. 'No,' he repeated, 'not simple-minded. In fact, a man to be watched.'

'Is that what you're doing — watching me?'

'Not at all,' Lansley protested. 'Well . . . only partly. I'm here to *help* Ward. When I learned you were investigating a marine insurance matter and coming to Alicante—'

'How did you discover that?'

Lansley kissed the girl's shoulder lightly: she was almost a head taller than he and as she looked down at him her smile seemed genuine, if edged with professionalism. 'You have to remember,' Lansley said softly, 'when one is . . . exiled as I am, living in a small town, among a boating fraternity, so many expatriates, gossip is rife. The *Sea Dawn* broke down not too far from Javea, before she proceeded on her voyage and went to the bottom. There were stories at the Yachting Club . . . and then, when news came to me from Newcastle that *you* were involved, that you'd engaged a London firm of marine investigators, I knew it would be only a matter of time before you would fly out here. What a chance for me to resume an acquaintance, meet again a man I admire!'

'You've explained little, Lansley. You took me by surprise at the airport, and nothing you've said makes sense since. I can't believe you are merely offering to help me out of a basic need to express yourself philanthropically.'

'Beautifully put, my friend, but I assure you—'

'No assurances, Lansley, just the truth.'

Lansley eased himself away from the girl; Elaine, practised in acceptance of such dismissals, moved towards the bar, making herself inconspicuous.

'The truth?' The fat man shook his head regretfully. There are so many truths. But one truth is that I find marine investigations a fascinating field of study. The law has got itself in such a mess, even though it's had so much time to sort itself out. I mean, did you know that in Demosthenes's *Orations Against Zemothemis* there is included an account of a plot to scuttle a ship in order to make off with the insurance monies?'

'I didn't,' Eric said grimly.

'It's true. An early form of marine insurance existed in Rome in 215 BC, and it quickly led to senators arranging for wrecks: it was a means of defrauding the state. And nothing has changed. Insuring a vessel and arranging for its total loss has never fallen out of fashion as a fraud, and is particularly favoured during times of economic recession, when there is the prospect of greater income from insurance than from lawful trade.'

'Are we talking about the *Sea Dawn*?'

Lansley's eyes widened in injured innocence. 'Would I be talking specifically? What do I know of the *Sea Dawn*? I merely gossip, observe, make a point. It is a common understanding among the fraternity that insurance companies and underwriters generally find it easier to pay losses than fight claimants. After all, faced with little or no evidence of the circumstances of the loss, an unfavourable burden of proof, and a high standard of proof, is not their attitude understandable? Which makes me curious as to why you are prepared to avoid this way out and tread the long and heavy road to prove a criminal act in the matter of the *Sea Dawn*.'

'You say you're generalizing, Lansley, but we never stray too far from the *Sea Dawn* herself.'

'But such an interesting case. Loss of only one life at the time, ship and cargo completely lost, odd circumstances relating to an engine breakdown off Denia—'

'And the master going ashore.'

'Quite.' Lansley smiled and sipped his wine. 'And then there's the fate of the master.'

'Olsen's are an efficient firm.'

'They've pointed me firmly in a certain direction.'

'Which is why you are here.' Lansley nodded. 'Well, of course, if there's any way in which I can help . . .'

'Why should you?'

'Don't be so suspicious, dear boy. Accept the sincerity of my offer. I'm an old, retired, ill Englishman, lonely for the sound of a northern accent, desirous of obtaining at a distance, and vicariously, a little of the excitement and passion that would be critical to his state of health if he were to experience it personally. I have no stake in this business of yours, Ward, but I'm fascinated by the process of its unravelling. I mean, this man Trainor . . .'

'The master of the Sea Dawn.'

'That's right. You will have been told he died.'

'In a car crash, outside Paris.'

'Indeed. But did you know a man was held by the police, to be charged with negligent driving and causing the death of the said Fred Trainor? And did you know that somehow he was able to spirit himself away? Disappeared from custody? And in the desultory inquiries thereafter, although the flies had his name, they were unable to prevent him slipping into Switzerland and obscurity.'

Eric stared at Lansley. 'You know the man's name?'

'The killer of Trainor? Yes. He's called Nicholas Bailey. He has something of a violent background.'

'How do you—'

'I have contacts,' Lansley stated blandly.

* * *

Halliday Arthur Lansley refused to be drawn further before they had eaten. The meal was a splendid one, as Eric could have guessed: built like a gourmand, Lansley had the tastes of a gourmet. The lobster was delicious, the emperador succulent, the pastry of the vol-au-vent light as air. Though he took little of the selection of wine — the dry Sancerre, the creamy Paillard Brut and the deep-coloured Pommard — Eric was aware it would be the apogee of top estate bottling. Lansley's conversation was witty and sparkling, he bestowed genuine affection verbally upon his girl companion, and towards Eric he behaved like a perfect host. As .they slipped through the darkness and the night air was warm about them Eric began to relax, even though he knew the danger of relaxation in Lansley's company: the man was a rogue, a confidence trickster whose word meant nothing. But he had charm.

But later, in the subdued light of the wheelhouse, Lansley himself had relaxed, soothed by good wine and good food, the prospect of the soft body of the girl in the cabin, and lulled by the swing of *La Encantada* and the luminescent sheen of the waters under the moon. He lit a cigar, exhaled with a satisfied gusto, and smiled.

'So you will need help. You'll wish to find out why Trainor came ashore when the *Sea Dawn* broke down.'

'I'll need to talk to Cordóbes, the Spanish agent for the Storcaster underwriters. It was he whom Trainor might have spent some time with.'

'It's possible.'

'And I need to find out more about the owners of the *Sea Dawn*. Brandon Roskill.'

'Madrid.' Lansley paused. 'You'll find out little there, I would guess. I have heard they have effectively gone into liquidation.'

'Before settlement of the claim?'

'Arrangements have been made,' Lansley said vaguely.

He moved to stand over the flickering lights of the sonar, his blotchy skin glowing eerily in the subdued luminescence as he watched the thick black continuous streaks that appeared on the sonar, intimating the presence of fish under the hull. 'I don't think you'll get much from Cordóbes, and you will be chasing rainbows if you go to Madrid, pursuing Brandon Roskill. On the other hand . . .'

'Yes?'

'There is a man . . . He is called Ruiz. He lives high in the mountains, at Guadalest. Now, from him you might get some interesting information.'

'What has he to do with the Sea Dawn?' Eric frowned. 'Was he a member of the crew?'

Lansley turned from the sonar, and his sparse hair seemed to shine against the background of flickering light. 'A crew member? No. Just a clerk. A humble clerk, in Marseilles.' Eric suspected the old man was smiling cynically as he added, 'In fact, to be precise, a simple shipping tally clerk.'

* * *

The morning sun was bright and sharp and the sky azure blue. The mountains were etched in a rugged line across his horizon, black in the sunlight, but their peaks tipped with gold as the rising sun sought out their hollows. Behind him, as he drove his hired Seat towards Jalón, the land stretched flatly towards the coast and the urgent jutting of the hill they called Montgo, towering protectively above Javea and its yacht-thronged port.

It was to the port that Lansley had brought him. They had moored in the harbour below Cabo San Antonio and had driven up the hillside to the white-walled villa behind the heavy doors: from its terrace Lansley enjoyed a sweeping view across the old town, the glittering stretch of sand at Arenal, and out to the islands at Cabo la Nao. The villa was spacious, beautifully appointed in Spanish hardwood style and completely private, screened by high walls covered in bougainvillea in shades of purple and red. They reflected a splash of colour in the deep blue water of the swimming pool and the sounds of the beach and the town below were a hazy murmur on the warm afternoon air.

Lansley had been correct in his advice to Eric. Contact with the Storcaster agent, Cordóbes, had been a waste of time. The office had been cool, air-conditioned although small, and Cordóbes, a neat, wiry man with intelligent eyes and a quick smile, had seemed helpful and eager to please.

It had been a mood which had quickly evaporated. His impression must have been that Eric wanted details of the Sea Dawn charter-party; once he learned that Eric wanted to talk about Fred Trainor and the first mate Mueller the intelligence in his eyes turned to diffidence and the smile changed into a stubborn lack of knowledge. He had certainly met Trainor, and when the engine breakdown had occurred Trainor had reported the matter to him and asked him to advise on the matter of repairs in Denia. He had mentioned several firms but he was unclear which had been selected. When Eric pointed out the firm was named in depositions placed before the court he had shrugged and said he had forgotten: the firm had in any case since been wound up, its principals moved away from Javea. As for the possibility of Trainor having talked with anyone else in the town while he was ashore during the repairs, he had no information regarding this: he was agent for Storcaster, not the handholder of ships' captains, and he had other clients apart from Storcaster, too

Eric was left with the impression that Cordóbes was being deliberately evasive. He could not be sure the man had any information of significance to give, but what he did have he was keeping to himself. He did not want to help Eric, and there was the likelihood he was acting on instructions from Berckman, Daniels and Germaine. They, as partners in the Storcaster Syndicate, had no interest in seeing Eric's path smoothed, now that Leonard Channing had thrown down the gauntlet to Eric in their presence.

Lansley had certainly saved Eric a trip to Madrid. He made some telephone inquiries from the villa: his uncertain Spanish caused some difficulties, but he learned enough to confirm what Lansley had told him: Brandon Roskill had certainly been liquidated, only a matter of months ago. The business had been wound up, but Eric was unable to contact anyone who could inform him how the company assets had been distributed, or to whom the rights in action outstanding — including the Sea Dawn insurance claim — had been assigned.

He felt angry and frustrated by his lack of progress, and as he stood on the balcony overlooking the swimming pool, watching Elaine and a tall blonde girl who had joined her swimming naked below him, his frustration turned to a muted anger. He could hear Lansley, out of sight in the shade of the balcony chuckling about something, and he knew that the second girl had been procured as a temptation to himself, a subtle gift there for the taking. As he watched her slim body in the deep blue water he was reminded of another time and place, a girl called Catherine who had swum with him and who had come in his room in the darkness. Lansley's methods did not change: his gifts were simple and direct. But on that last occasion he had wanted something from Eric and had used him deliberately: what did he want from Eric now?

Eric had turned away and placed a phone call to Reuben Podmore. It had been a bad time: frustrated, impatient and angry with himself for the stirring of his body, he had been m no mood to weigh up important considerations and take decisions. Podmore had been explicit.

'Yes, Mr Ward, I've made the contacts. As you predicted, not too many eyebrows are being raised. When I put out some feelers with the brokers it was clear they assumed that Martin and Channing were thinking of playing some deep game only they needed to know about. They will clearly be happy to allow Stanley Investments to pick up some of the Eurobond issue.'

'And have you made the commitment?'

'As I've already explained to you, Mr Ward, it's not a good time. It's true the market has moved to the appropriate level for the moment—'

'Can you buy in at nine and a half?'

'I can, but I really must try to impress upon you that the time is not a good one. The omens—'

'You can't take business decisions based on superstition, Podmore.'

'The omens,' Podmore had insisted, his voice crackling unhappily over the phone, 'are not good. The rates are fluctuating so wildly at this time, the oil talks in OPEC are causing flutterings in London, the Paris security scare could well hit confidence at the Bourse, and the period really is one for retrenchment rather than foolish speculation.'

'But you can buy in at nine and a half.'

'Yes — but really, Mr Ward . . .'

Eric took a deep breath, half exasperation, half relief. 'Do it, Podmore.'

'This kind of decision, at this time—'

'Do it!'

When he had replaced the phone, Eric Ward had felt hollow inside.

* * *

It had been a relief, early next morning, to leave the villa and take the road south-west into the mountains. In the foothills he passed small scattered villages: it would have been faster to take the motorway south towards Calpe and then join the tourist tracks winding up through the hills to the ancient village of Guadalest, but he had chosen to take the more direct, if slower and more winding road, through Jalón and straight up over the jagged peaks.

It was certainly a more picturesque road, even if it did demand greater concentration on driving. He had the car windows right down, for even though he was climbing high on a winding road that twisted and zigzagged along valley and hillsides, the air was already hot from the bright sun. As he climbed, vineyards and olive groves and acres of orange trees spread out below him, while the wind whipped up dust clouds on the roadway ahead at the peaks.

The road was quiet. A mile or so below him another car climbed lazily, and he had passed two small convoys of vehicles coming down from Jalón. The one group consisted of a procession of three farm vehicles, a family eking out a living in the high sierra land. The second convoy caused him momentary trouble: four beach buggies tearing around the narrow peak road, too fast, too full and too careless. The first missed him by inches with a cacophonous blasting of horns: he was able to slow and edge in to the side of the road as the others careered past. He looked down — at the drop they would have faced if they had collided with him and could not prevent the involuntary shudder. They were young and found the speed exciting: perhaps when you thought about the dangers, you were getting old. He hoped the red car climbing below him would meet them on a straight stretch of road.

Inside the hour he had crossed the first range of peaks, wound down into the valley below past Tarbena and was on the road to Guadalest. When he joined the main road leading up from the coast he met the inevitable cluster of coaches, packed with white-faced tourists. He managed to squeeze past a couple of them on a straight stretch of road, but was then forced to curb his impatience as he straggled along behind a yellow and gold monstrosity which crawled across the narrow roads above the ravines and ground its way towards the village on the peak.

He could see Guadalest when he was still two miles distant. The white watchtower and the church sparkled in the sunshine, perched on the naked rock, high above the plunging scarp slope to the valley below, drowned by the long finger of the manmade lake. He overtook the coach at last, sped along the rising gradient till he reached the turning to the parking area, and quickly found a space — and an attendant waiting to be paid.

Halliday Arthur Lansley had given him an address. Eric made his way across the car park past the restaurant and climbed the steps leading up to the rock face and the tunnel carved centuries ago to give the only access to the fortified village on the peak. The steps were bounded by shops cluttered with scarves and leather goods and souvenirs sought by tourists. He ignored them, and with the sun hot on the back of his neck he paced up the twisting steps, walked through the coolness of the tunnel and found himself in the main street of the village, called, oddly enough for a single, narrow, stepped street leading up the hillside, the *Plaza del Caudillo.*

The street was festooned with banners, *Guadalest en Festes*, and thronged with tourists who had poured from the coaches parked below in the square and the upmarket shops. Shop fronts yawned darkly at him but he ignored their temptations: he checked the numbers of the doorways until he found the one he wanted. There was a woman seated on a cane chair in the entrance to the *pueblo.* She was in her sixties, but her skin was like parchment, dried and wrinkled as she squinted up at him in the warm morning sunlight. She had been working on a lace mantilla, presumably for the tourist trade, but her hands were still now in her lap as she stared at him expectantly.

'*Buenas dias . . .*' Eric struggled for the words. '*Quisiero . . . puedo vis tar Señor Ruid.*'

She stared at him uncomprehendingly, and then dropped her glance to the stained rusty black of her dress. Eric tried again with his halting, ungrammatical Spanish. As he spoke, she kept her head down.

'*Dondi esta Señor Ruid Quiero . . .*'

He repeated his halting request and at last something seemed to get through to her. He was searching for a man called Ruiz; he had been told that Senor Ruiz lived in this house, had come back to retire here in the mountain village he had left many years before to work at sea, beyond the sierra. The woman stared at him and her eyes were liquid as she suddenly leaned forward and gestured with her hand, pointing up the Plaza del Caudillo to the tiny square that crowned the village.

Something cold moved in Eric's stomach.

He thanked her dully, and walked up the hill. The famed 'eagle's nest' fortress of Guadalest, built by the Moors over a thousand years ago, and inaccessible except for the tunnel carved through fifty feet of solid rock, had never been conquered. From the tiny square Eric could see why: eyries of outposts on soaring rock pinnacles protected it; the walls were built on top of the sheer-faced crag; the fearsome drop below fell hundreds of feet over rock and shale and scrambling slopes on which an enemy would never obtain a foothold. It had had to be self-sufficient if it was to withstand siege, so it had its own church and belfry, perched on a pinnacle, and its own prison for recalcitrance.

It also had its own burial ground.

Eric walked across the square and past the ancient prison.

He climbed the twisting steps, hardly aware as he doubled back on himself of the spreading vista of the knife-edged sierra slicing upwards to the sky above the manmade lake below, an iridescent blue against the pale grey mud of its dehydrated banks. He climbed to the high point of the crag and the gates of the tiny memorial garden were in front of him, a scattering of dusty flowers in bulbous brown pots.

To his left were two walls in which glass-windowed apertures appeared. Some of the apertures were sealed: two had been cemented over. Behind the glass were statements and photographs: dully, Eric stared at them, wondering inconsequentially why the photographs that had been chosen were always of the deceased in old age. Perhaps to display youth above the ashes would have been deemed an obscenity.

He found the space he was looking for near the top of the wall on the right. There was no likeness of Arturo Ruiz. The words were freshly painted in gold leaf. He had been sixty-two years old. He had been cremated and interred here barely two weeks ago.

Recuerdo de sus hijos.

Eric stared at the sombre words. His drive to Guadalest had been a waste of time. He had come too late. Whatever the simple tally clerk from Marseilles might have been able to tell him about the loss of the *Sea Dawn* had been burned with the man himself.

Unless Halliday Arthur Lansley knew more than he was telling.

Thoughtfully, Eric made his way back to the car. He didn't trust Lansley: the man was quite capable of sending Eric on a wild goose chase, but Eric had no idea what the motivation behind it might have been. He supposed it was possible that Lansley had not known Ruiz was dead apparently of natural causes — but Lansley's boast about his sources of information would suggest he *should* have known. If that was the case, why had he sent Eric up into the Sierra de Serreta?

Eric backed the car out of his parking space and drove down into the bend that would take him back down the road to Callosa and the coast. He felt angry, eager to see Lansley again, have it out with him, but the anger was muted by a vague sense of unease. Two of the coaches had pulled out ahead of him and he chugged along behind them gloomily as they crept their way around the sharp bends and crossed the ravine of the Rio Guadalest.

He guessed he would be stuck behind them most of the way down to the coast road, so once he reached Callosa he decided to swing back again on the mountain road that would lead him up to Tarbena and over the Coll de Rates, fifteen hundred feet above the plains of oranges and vines that swept down to Denia and the coast. It was the route Lansley had earlier recommended, so Eric took it once again.

He barely concentrated on the road ahead and was unmindful of the craggy scenery as he wound his way up to Tarbena. He barely noticed the terraced slopes and the groves of gnarled olive trees: his mind was confused, the puzzle of Lansley's appearance at Alicante merging with the reluctance of Cordóbes to talk to him and the useless pursuit of information from the tally clerk Ruiz in Guadalest. He felt he was losing his way, missing the connecting points, following blind leads that left him disorientated. He was no longer entirely sure what he had hoped to achieve in coming to Spain, or even in consulting Olsen in the matter of the *Sea Dawn* investigation.

At the El Algar waterfalls Eric pulled in and took a break.

His head was beginning to ache, with a tell-tale prickling at the back of his eyes that presaged pain, arising from tension and anxiety. He parked and walked to the eighty-foot falls. He stared at them moodily, hardly aware of the scattering of tourists about him, asking himself angrily what he was trying to prove. An arbitration and a court of justice had mulled over the facts of the sinking of the *Sea Dawn*; an experienced Commissioner of Wrecks had adjudicated upon the issues. If they had not asked the questions Eric thought they should have asked it might have been because their experience told them it was useless, or time-wasting, to ask such questions. Answers might lie at the bottom of the Mediterranean, but it was unlikely they could get dredged to the surface in a judicial inquiry.

The key, Eric decided, lay with Leonard Channing. He was forced to admit to himself that if Channing had not made a fool of him it was unlikely that Eric himself would have then proceeded with the stubborn refusal to pay off the Storcaster Syndicate. And as for the underwriting of the Deutsche Bank Eurobond issue . . .

He walked back to his car, and drove away, up the steep winding road to the Coll de Rates. He came up over the top and the vista spread out in front of him: the line of foothills barring him from the coast and the distant blue of the sea barely discernible in the shimmering heat haze. The road ahead dipped in a series of hairpin bends, some wide and sweeping, some tight and cramped as they crossed narrow gullies that would be awash with fierce streams during the winter rains, whipping past the craggy limestone rocks and outcrops greened with silver-leaved olive trees. At the foot of the road lay Parcent, sprawling in a bowl of the hillside, a white-walled village crowned with a dazzling church tower on the hill, dominating the scene about it.

But not from here, not from the Coll de Rates. There was the scent of pine in Eric's nostrils as he eased the car forward over the craggy peak to begin the long descent to the town below, to Jalón's orange groves, and to Javea.

Where Halliday Arthur Lansley would be waiting.

* * *

He cruised over the top and began the long winding descent, braking before the bends, accelerating gently into them, aware of the steep drop beyond the concrete blocks that had been placed at the road edge to prevent an accidental plunging over. As he came down the hill he changed into third gear to negotiate a bend: a tractor came chugging around ahead of him and the farmer behind the wheel raised a hand in greeting. Eric responded as the man drove past, then glanced in the mirror to glimpse the tractor moving around the bend behind him.

He caught a flash of red before he himself was turning into the next bend.

The road straightened and levelled out for three hundred metres, before the stomach-dropping descent towards Parcent appeared ahead, the road twisting whitely back upon itself, shimmering and dancing in the sunshine while Parcent glittered at the road's end. Eric glanced in his wing mirror and saw the red car swing around the bend behind him, accelerating down the hill, and grimaced: someone was eager to get to the bottom of the mountain, or else was out to impress. He slowed, uncertain whether the driver wanted to pass before the next hairpin but the red car stationed itself some fifty metres back. Eric took the bend, accelerating out of it and the road straightened again, leaving a four-hundred-metre stretch of coasting down the hill, time for the red Ford behind him to gun its engine and overtake with style.

The car edged closer, but made no attempt to pass.

Eric slowed, checked his wing mirror, then beckoned the driver behind, inviting him to overtake.

The Ford kept station, edging nearer, slightly out towards the crown of the road and getting a little too close for comfort.

Eric frowned in annoyance, and then shook his head, picked up speed and pulled away slightly from the Ford. It was only when he glanced in his rear mirror and saw that the Ford had crept closer again that the warning bells began to sound.

He changed gear at the end of the stretch. The road looped whitely ahead of him, shimmering in the hot morning sun, and as it almost doubled back on itself it ran into a clump of pine trees fringing the craggy drop of cliff, plunging two hundred feet down to a rocky outcrop below. Eric swung into the bend, aware he needed to take the centre of the road to stay away from the unguarded edge of a precipitous drop, and as he did so he caught out of the corner of his eye the movement of red in the mirror.

'Crazy bastard!' Eric said to himself, as he saw the driver positioning himself to overtake. There had been no sign of a vehicle ahead climbing the mountain, but the driver of the Ford could not be certain the track ahead was without obstruction. His line of vision was more limited than Eric's and the swing of the bend would inevitably make overtaking a hazardous operation. Eric slowed, cursing the Ford but giving the driver his chance.

He did not take it. Instead, as Eric slowed, the Ford came thrusting forward in a sudden violent acceleration and its nose thundered in the rear of Eric's vehicle. He was thrown forward, his hands slipping from the wheel and the Seat lurched, swinging wildly away from the centre of the road, heeling across to the edge of the dusty track. His tyres hit gravel and sandy earth, spraying grit high out over the edge of the precipice and Eric caught a brief glimpse of the rocky slope falling away to his right as he pulled the bucking wheel sideways and the Seat began to swing, out of control in a series of lurching, shuddering curves down the hillside.

He slammed hard on the brakes but immediately realized his error as the car went into a skid, sliding towards the cliff wall to his right. He struck the cliff with a glancing blow that sent the vehicle careering outwards again: Eric steered with the skid, instinct and training from the police school years ago reasserting itself. The Seat veered crazily inwards again, then steadied as he pulled out to the right-hand side of the road to pick up the natural curve of the bend. It lasted only for yards: almost before Eric had a chance to glance in the mirror and curse the Ford its bonnet shuddered into him again.

For a moment everything seemed frozen. He was staring in the rear mirror and he could see the man's face: dark hair, eyes hidden behind dark glasses, mouth open as though he was shouting something. Then Eric braked hard, realizing that the Ford behind was being deliberately used as a weapon of aggression, that the man intended running him off the road, and the best thing was to stop, pull in to the side even if there was the danger of a car coming up the hill and ploughing into him. He was safer on the cliff wall side than teetering on the precipitous edge. He braked again, wrenching the wheel across.

It almost worked. It would have worked, he knew, if the man behind hadn't been expecting it. At the first braking he also had slowed; as Eric braked again, dragging the car across to the cliff wall there was a momentary hesitation and then the Ford driver gunned his engine, throwing the car at Eric's Seat and catching it at an angle, sliding the vehicle away from the wall, at an angle across the road to the cliff edge.

In split seconds the Seat would be over the edge. Eric reacted instinctively, slamming down hard on the accelerator and regaining control of the bucking Seat, breaking free from the thrust of the Ford momentarily, and careering forward again, dangerously close to the edge as the road levelled out but away from the hammering of the car behind. Ahead of him the road straightened momentarily, and then began a slow curve again into a series of sharp bends which Eric recalled would spiral down some four hundred feet to the valley floor before it rose again to cross a small ravine by a narrow bridge. He accelerated into the bend, caught another glimpse of the charging red Ford and guessed he'd be lucky ever to reach the ravine bridge alive.

The Ford hit him again with even greater force than before, jerking his head back painfully, rattling his teeth, and he grabbed at the wheel, held it grimly against the strain of the bend as he felt the vehicle lift, perilously close to cartwheeling sideways and plunging to the oblivion of the rocky slope below. He slammed the gears into second and hit the accelerator hard: the extra control and the slower surge helped him hold the bend and as the Ford came screaming forward, buckling the rear panel of the Seat completely, Eric changed up again, hammering the vehicle forward into the bend, gaining a sudden fifteen-yard gap before the Ford driver could react. But it was a matter of seconds only: the more powerful Ford was gunned forward again, seeking the Seat, determined to thrust it crashing over the edge. Eric forced the car out of the bend, pushed his own engine with his foot flat to the floorboards, to lessen the impact of the inevitable charge of the Ford.

Then, at the last moment, as both cars were screaming with smoking tyres around the sharp curve Eric wrenched the wheel to the left and stood on his brakes, grabbing his handbrake fiercely at the same time. The Seat decelerated sharply, the nose swung in a tight arc first heading for the cliff wall and then gathering momentum in its swing to almost face back up the hill as its rear was hit by the Ford.

Taken by surprise, the Ford driver never stood any chance of correcting the situation. As the Seat swung broadside to him and he roared forward the nose of his car struck Eric's a glancing blow. The surge of his own engine did the rest. Without the weight of the Seat to slow him, and the glancing blow sliding him outwards to the right from the curve of the bend there was no opportunity to correct the slide. He must have dragged at the wheel, and his brake lights glowed red, but it was all too sharp and too late. His tyres hit the sandy edge of the roadway, the battered nose of the Ford lifted, bucking and gleaming in the hot sunlight and then with a coughing roar that suddenly turned into a high, whining sound the car seemed to launch itself into space, sailing majestically forward until its momentum slowed and it began to describe an impossibly ugly parabola, its nose dipping, its rear wheels rising and throwing the whole vehicle into a cartwheeling motion that lost it to Eric's line of sight in seconds.

The Seat was still sliding across the road to the cliff face.

It struck with a resounding, shuddering blow that killed the engine as Eric was jerked sideways in his seat. But the air was not silent. As his own car shuddered to a halt Eric could hear the crashing, bouncing sound of screaming metal and shattering glass, the thunder of the noise picked up in echoing ravines, repeated over and over, almost endlessly it seemed, whispering into the far hills like a distant storm warning.

Slowly, an eerie silence came to the hill. The blood was thundering in Eric's ears, a pounding in his head that was like a series of physical blows. He pushed at his car door; it refused to open at his first attempts but when he thrust his shoulder against it, it lurched wide and he half fell out of the driving seat.

The tick of cooling, strained metal was loud in the silence and the smell of burned rubber was strong in the air. Eric breathed deeply, focusing his blurred vision and then unsteadily he walked across the road, shaking his head to clear it. He stood at the edge and looked down.

A hundred and fifty feet below him on the mountainside the wrecked Ford lay crumpled on the craggy outcrop. Its back was broken, the roof collapsed, the chassis twisted and torn apart. There was no sign of movement, and no body on the rocks. The driver, Eric guessed, was still inside. It was unlikely he would have survived the fall.

Painfully, Eric stepped down from the road and began to scramble his way down the rocky scree towards the shattered car below. Eucalyptus bushes and wild rosemary grew in scattered clumps among the rocks and as he grasped at them for support he caught the scent of their crushed leaves in his nostrils.

Just fifty feet down the slope he caught another odour: spilled petrol.

He stopped, peering down the slope to the car. The sun picked up the glint of the liquid from the burst petrol tank, and even as he stood there Eric caught a glimpse of the tiny flicker of flame emerging from the shattered bonnet of the Ford. Rooted to the spot, he was motionless for almost a minute, uncertain what to do: the flames were more vigorous suddenly, feeding off the hot oil and then, as though they had been lifted by a soft breeze they crept their red, uncertain way past the crazily hanging door of the passenger seat and in a sudden confident flurry picked up the dripping petrol, running with a soft *whooshing* sound to blaze up around the broken wheels.

Eric stayed where he was. He knew now that whoever was inside the car stood no chance: if he was not already dead, as was likely, he would suffocate or be burned to death in a matter of seconds, long before Eric could reach him. As for Eric, if he did not step back there was the danger he could be caught by the inevitable explosion.

Slowly he scrambled back up the roadway. It was several minutes before the explosion came. When it did, scraps of burning rubber were hurled into the air and the ravines echoed again to thunder.

Eric stood dumbly at the side of the road, staring down.

He saw little. His mind was numbed, and yet something crawled coldly inside him, a slow uncurling of anger. The man down there had tried to kill him and had died himself in the attempt. His motives were unknown to Eric, but he could make a fair guess that it was certainly connected with a fat man in a villa above Javea old town.

He had been set up. He had been sent on a wild goose chase into the mountains. It was Halliday Arthur Lansley who had sent him, suggesting the quieter route, and put him into a position where he would be open to attack on the lonely country road above Jalón. The surprise thrust should have sent him to oblivion. It hadn't, but the man who had died had been told where he was to be. Eric Ward had been set up by the exiled confidence trickster from *La Encantada*.

He walked back to the car thoughtfully, the cold knot of anger hardening, curling unpleasantly inside him. His cheekbone felt sore; there was a superficial wound on his forehead though he had no recollection of striking his head, and there was a soreness about his shoulder and neck muscles. His left hand was painful, the knuckles swollen and puffy.

If the man below had had his say in it, things would have been a lot more serious.

Eric got into the car, slipped the gear into neutral and tried to start the engine. The starter motor whined and died. He sat in the driving seat and tried again, cursing under his breath. He had no wish to attempt the long walk down the mountainside, and inevitable explanations if he was picked up by a passing motorist.

The car refused to start. Frustrated, he got out and walked to the edge of the road, scanning the country below him. There was a brief, glinting flash of sunlight: a car was making its slow, grinding way up the bends towards him. In perhaps fifteen minutes it would pass the spot where he stood: then, or at some point earlier, it would see the wrecked Ford on the crag.

Eric went back to his car. He twisted the key again, the engine almost caught. Savagely he tried the motor once more and sluggishly it responded. There was a long, breath-taking moment when he thought the surge would die again and then the engine thundered to life, power roaring noise against the hill as he pumped at the accelerator, and slammed the driver's door shut beside him.

He edged the Seat forward, turning it bumpily, reversing it into a clumsy three-point turn until he was facing back down the mountain. He slipped into second gear and coasted his way down into the bend, away from the shattered wreck to his right.

He had an appointment to keep with Halliday Arthur Lansley. Behind him the thick, oily plume of smoke ascended lazily in the clear mountain air.

* * *

The two girls had been dismissed. Reluctantly, they had emerged from the pool and dressed in bathrobes, then sauntered away into the villa. Lansley had ignored them as he sat in the shade, his enormous paunch hanging over the waist of his Bermuda shorts, the blotchy skin of his shoulders pink and unhealthy-looking against the bronzed, muscled arms of the man who stood just to one side and behind him. The man's face was impassive, but the eyes beneath the heavy eyebrows were watchful. When Eric had finally been admitted to the villa, the soft-footed, athletically-built manservant had stood close to one side of him. Now, once the girls had been dismissed he had moved beside Lansley, watching Eric, his upper body seemingly relaxed but the muscles of his calves tense, as though he was ready to spring forward if Eric made a physical move against the fat man. 'Well,' Lansley said slowly, 'maybe now we can talk a bit more rationally. I don't like people coming into my home in the . . . ah . . . obvious anger you've been displaying.'

'You bastard!'

'Mr Ward—'

'You set me up!'

'From your appearance,' Lansley said in a cool tone, 'you appear to have walked down from Guadalest, and by the most direct route. I take it from your . . . discontent, you did not meet Ruiz?'

'He's dead — as you damn well knew before you sent me up into the sierra.'

Lansley's eyes widened for a moment. He reached out to the table-top beside him and picked up his long glass of gin and tonic. The ice clinked softly as he shook the glass in a gentle motion. 'Manuel?' he said quietly.

The man behind him stirred uneasily, glanced briefly away from Eric and replied, 'We had no report, *Señor*.'

Lansley's little eyes flickered a hostile glance up to Eric. 'My sources in England are busy and reliable and numerous. They are also trustworthy. Networks in Spain are more . . . unreliable. You tell me Ruiz is dead.'

'Several days ago. He's been cremated. Don't tell me you didn't know.'

'Natural causes?' Lansley asked wonderingly.

'It would seem so. Your henchman died more violently, however.'

Lansley was silent for almost a minute. He stared at Eric, taking in the detail of his dishevelled state, the scalp wound, the dark swelling on his left hand. 'My henchman . . . I'm not sure you know what you're saying, my friend. An explanation is in order, I think—'

'Yes. From you.'

Lansley sipped his gin and tonic. His eyes glinted; his temper was beginning to rise. He was not used to being talked to like this in his own home. He put the glass down on the table. 'You'd better tell me what happened, Ward. I assure you, I don't know what you're talking about—'

'The hell you don't!' Eric interrupted crisply. 'You set me up. You sent me up to Guadalest, knowing that Ruiz was dead. You got me away to a quiet road in the sierra where I could be forced over the edge, where maybe it would be expected I'd have had an *accident*. But it didn't work out that way, and you've got a hell of a lot of explaining to do. A wreck on the mountainside, a dead man — when I talk to the police about it, you'd better get your story straight. But what I want to know is *why*!'

Lansley grimaced, drawing his pudgy lips back over his teeth in a gesture of irritation. 'Details. Give me the details,' he insisted.

Eric hesitated, glaring angrily at the fat man facing him.

He had been fooled by Lansley before and he did not intend that it should happen again. His glance slipped to the impassive, heavily-muscled man standing watchfully just behind Lansley: when Eric had driven down from the mountains it had been with anger in his veins. The anger was still with him, but it was colder, more controlled. 'All right,' he said. 'Details.' He told Lansley of the drive into the mountains, taking the route Lansley had suggested. He told him of the discovery of the death of Ruiz, the man Lansley had told him to visit. He told him of the loneliness of the high road and the way the man in the red Ford had come thrusting out of the bend to try to drive him over the edge. And he made it clear, as he gave Lansley the account, that he regarded the man from Newcastle as the person responsible for ordering the attack.

'Interesting,' Lansley said, almost in a whisper. His lips seemed dry: his little pink tongue darted out several times, massaging the fleshy mouth. 'But you jump to conclusions.'

'Lansley—'

'If I had wanted you killed there are methods, believe me, that I would have employed . . . far more discreet, even if less dramatic, than trying to drive you off a mountain road. And probably more effective.' He held out his glass: the man behind him moved with alacrity to fill it. 'I need time, to think, and to get a few answers. Did you see the man behind you in the car?'

'Are you joking? He was trying to kill me! I wasn't particularly interested in seeing his face — I was trying to keep that damned Seat on the road.'

'Yes. Of course.' Lansley hardly appeared to be listening, as he churned images inside his skull, sweating lightly, and puffing his fat cheeks. 'Yes . . . The car, it is hired. That can be left to me. We will make arrangements, no questions . . . And the man who attacked you . . . it is certain he is dead?'

'I saw no body on the rocks, and no one could have survived the wreck, and the explosion.'

'All right.' Lansley nodded, satisfied. 'We will set it all in order. You say there was a car climbing the hill after the . . . incident?'

'I imagine the wreck will have been seen and reported by now.'

'But there is nothing to connect you with the . . . accident, except your battered car. We will talk to certain people—'

'What the hell are you suggesting?'

Lansley sipped his wine for a few moments then regarded Eric owlishly. He shook his head. 'Mr Ward, an attempt has just been made on your life. The car you drove was severely damaged. There has been a fatal result to the . . . encounter. You did not go to the police.'

'I was angry, and I knew you'd set me up—'

'But you did not go to the police. That is the important point. If you go how, questions of all kinds will be asked. Not only of you, but of me, too. That would be . . . unfortunate. It would be easier, therefore, if you left matters in my hands so that I may make arrangements—'

'You intend hushing matters up? Look here, Lansley—'

'I repeat, Mr Ward, you have already compromised yourself. Do you know what the inside of a gaol is like? I do. I did not like the experience. And a Spanish gaol . . . I believe I would lack certain essential creature comforts. No, you may have acted rashly in coming straight here to the villa from your experience on the road from Guadalest, but you acted wisely, nevertheless. It is important now that you leave everything in my hands—'

'You've already set me up once—'

'If I had, you would not be alive here now!' Lansley flashed at him, irritated. 'It's best now we move with circumspection. I need time to make a few calls, talk to a few people, ensure that the matter is treated as a complete accident, for there is nothing to be gained any other way.'

'I'm not sure I can accept—'

'You lack choice in the matter, Ward,' Lansley said coldly and heaved himself to his feet. He turned to the man he had called Manuel and spoke to him rapidly in an undertone. His Spanish was too swift for Eric to follow. The manservant gestured towards Eric as he replied and Lansley shook his head, taking the man by the elbow and almost thrusting him away. Then he turned back to Eric.

'I must go out now. There are people to see. It is not an easy matter, disposing of this affair, but it can be done. Equally important, I must have time to get the answers I know you will now be demanding of me. I must request of you therefore a little patience.'

'I can't be party to a cover-up, Lansley.'

'I don't intend covering up anything in the way you suggest. First of all, I swear to you I did not arrange the incident in the mountains. Secondly, the only man we can reach at this stage is the man who lies dead up there above Jalón. There is nothing to be gained by police involvement. So you must leave things to me, and if you do not trust me—'

'*Ha!*'

'—then at least give me the benefit of a doubt, a little time, and I promise you we will speak at length, and I will attempt some explanation of the circumstances in which you find yourself — in so far as I am able to unravel them.'

'How much time?' Eric asked suspiciously.

'I will be as quick as I can. Now, please excuse me, for I must change.'

* * *

After the fat man had waddled away Eric went to the room Lansley had set aside for him and stripped, to take a cool shower and ease his bruised body. He lay on the bed for a couple of hours, letting the warm afternoon air dry him, and he fell into a light sleep that was punctuated by violent dreams of noise and fire and the smell of burning flesh. The afternoon lengthened and Eric stood on the balcony to his room: the pool was deserted and the villa was silent, but Eric knew Lansley would not have left him alone. The fat man had asked for time and had left the villa, but he would not have taken Eric entirely on trust.

Eric was puzzled. He had been foolish returning to the villa, and yet the action was probably the right thing to do, as Lansley had suggested. If Lansley had not been involved in the attack whoever wanted Eric dead would still be likely to want him out of the way, and the villa gave Eric a measure of protection. Moreover, Lansley was in a position to get answers where Eric could not: Lansley's connections with the European underworld were closer than Eric's by a long chalk. And little would have been gained by going to the police. They would certainly have been interested in an attempted murder, but Eric would have been able to give them little by way of information: not that they would have come to that conclusion for several days, he guessed.

Even so, he was uneasy at remaining here at the villa as Lansley's 'guest': it had overtones of menace he did not like. He tested them by dressing and leaving his room. He was met only feet from his door by another muscled, polite henchman who asked him if he would like something to eat. Eric settled for a cold drink and a seat beside the pool, in the shade.

There was only one way he would manage to leave the villa, and he did not relish the size of the manservant's muscles.

At seven thirty in the evening he was still on the pool terrace, alone. A light salad had been brought to him even though he had made no request: the bottle of Sangria had also been placed at his elbow unbidden. The sun was dropping in the sky and shadows were creeping across the town below, shading the blocks of apartments at Arenal beach and sending long dark fingers across the bright sand. He picked at the salad and poured himself a glass of Sangria. The ice tinkled in his glass and he held the glass against his heated forehead. He rose, walked impatiently around the pool and sipped the Sangria, checked his watch, and then went back inside the villa. There was a radio in the long lounge area: he switched it on.

It was several minutes before he picked up the news programme. He listened intently, concentrating hard to pick up the swift flow of the Spanish commentator. As far as Eric could make out there was no mention of a fatal car crash below the Coll de Rates; on the other hand, he could not be certain the programme contained details of local news. It could be a national network. The main items he picked up concerned the assassination of a political figure in New York, and the failure of an economic summit meeting in Paris, connected with the European money 'snake'. He turned off the radio, and thought for a while. After some hesitation he walked across to the telephone. Getting in touch with England was remarkably easy, and when Anne finally reached the phone it was almost as though she were in the next room.

'Darling! Are you all right over there?'

'Fine,' he lied. 'I was just ringing to tell you I'll try to get back home tomorrow. It's been a bit of a wild goose chase over here as far as I can see, and there's little to be gained by staying on. I'll have to check on flight times and reservations, so I'll ring again tomorrow when I've fixed something up.'

'That's a relief. Things have been bouncing back here.'

'About the *Sea Dawn* business?'

'The *Sea Dawn*? No, of course not, I know nothing much about all that.' She hesitated, and something in her tone changed. 'It's about Stanley Investments. I think you'd better get back here as fast as you can.'

'I don't understand.'

'Neither do I.'

Eric paused, and frowned. Anne's voice was cool, with an underlying tension apparent, perhaps heightened by the phone communication itself. 'You're talking in riddles, Anne.'

'I mean what I said. I don't understand, *can't* understand why you didn't explain to me what you were doing.'

'About what?'

'The Eurobond issue.'

He could hear her breathing at the other end of the phone; it had an agitated sound about it. He could not be certain whether she was angry or nervous. 'I explained to you what I was trying to do.'

'Not in detail. And not about the consequences.'

'You'd better tell me what's happened.'

'Podmore . . . he's been trying to get hold of you. He was getting agitated, but couldn't contact you at your hotel—'

'I didn't take up the reservation. I'm staying with an old friend,' Eric said grimly. 'What's bothering Podmore?'

'He wouldn't tell me at first. I pulled rank on him in the end and he cracked because he's worried sick, and as he says, it *is* my money.'

'That's right,' Eric said quietly, 'it's your money.'

She was silent for a few moments. 'I didn't mean it like that. And I did agree to what you were trying to do. But you didn't tell me it was *illegal!*'

'It isn't.'

'Well, all right, not exactly *illegal*, but Mark tells me it's sailing very close to the wind and all hell is breaking loose.' The ubiquitous Mark Fenham. Coolly Eric asked, 'Where does Fenham fit into this?'

'I went to him for advice. I told him what was bothering Podmore and Mark just about went up the wall. He told me you were crazy taking the chances you've done, and he advised me to see Leonard Channing right away—'

'*What?*'

'He argued that if I approached Channing maybe it could be sorted out before things got too bad—'

'Did you contact Channing?' Eric ground out.

'No, of course not, I wouldn't do that without talking it over first with you, but then things got worse and this morning Channing was on the phone to me—'

'How did he find out?'

There was a short silence. 'I suppose Mark . . .'

'*Bloody hell!*'

'Dammit, Eric, maybe I was wrong to go to him for advice but what the hell was I supposed to do with you out of touch, Podmore dancing around like a fat dervish worrying himself sick, and—'

'All right, all right.'

'And you can't even blame Mark, after all, not with the way things have gone.'

'What do you mean?'

'How out of touch are you?' she almost wailed. 'Haven't you heard the news?'

'I don't know what you're talking about.'

'Podmore's almost having a series of heart attacks. The economic summit collapse and this damned assassination has sent the money markets crazy. Podmore tells me he predicted to you there'd be problems, but with the international situation things have almost ground to a stop and the investment looks pretty bad. And Channing's been on the phone to him.'

'Go on.'

'He said you and Podmore could never have expected to get away with this . . .. *chicanery* was the word he used. The world of share wheeling and dealing is a small one and you could never have expected the buying in of the Eurobonds to remain a secret—'

'I hadn't expected Fenham to shout it from the housetops,' Eric said bitterly.

'I don't *know* that Mark told Channing,' Anne replied somewhat defensively. 'Anyway, the fact is Channing does know, he's breathing fire and he's threatened to sack Podmore.'

'That's not within his present jurisdiction. Tell Podmore not to worry.'

'Worry? He's panic-stricken. Not simply about the threat of the sacking. There's the whole ethical question — which he says he warned you about. He's very concerned about his reputation as an investment manager, and about the fact we're likely to be saddled with the Eurobond issue, which we will probably not be able to move except at a considerable loss.'

'With Channing putting the knives in as well.'

'That sums it up. It's as well you're coming home tomorrow.'

'To face the music?'

'Your words, Eric.'

'I'll be back as soon as I can, tomorrow.'

If Halliday Arthur Lansley allowed.

* * *

The fat man did not return to the villa until almost ten thirty that evening. Eric was still waiting in the lounge. He had had a salad and some fish earlier; when Lansley inquired whether he had eaten Eric was able to comment upon the hospitality that kept him well fed, albeit imprisoned. Lansley merely *humphed*, preoccupied; he poured himself a large Scotch, dumped his jacket on a chair and gestured to Eric to join him on the terrace.

The pool was lit and the water was a translucent, brilliant green, a rich colour that dappled the walls of the villa in contrast to the blue-black of the starlit sky. Lansley stood at the pool edge and stared down at the lights stringing the curve of Arenal beach as the lighthouse on Cabo San Antonio flickered its warning across the port and the darkened bay.

'Some evenings I stand here and look out to sea,' Lansley muttered moodily, 'and it's like there's no evil in the world.' It was men like Lansley who brought that evil to the surface, Eric thought. 'Have you settled the business of the car?' he asked.

Lansley nodded. 'I have. It cost me . . . but there'll be no comeback. And I've spoken to some people at Alicante, as well as Denia: there'll be no questions asked about the *accident* below the Coll de Rates. It'll go in the books as a drunken driver, a careless bit of driving, a burst tyre . . .'

'Identification?'

Lansley took a long pull at his Scotch and breathed deeply. 'That's never a difficulty. Papers and identities are not so difficult to come by. I've settled things with the police. An identity has been furnished. It will be non-threatening.'

'Do you know who the driver really was?'

'I do.'

'Well?'

Lansley hesitated for a short while, then he shrugged and turned. He walked back along the pool edge to the terrace and negotiated his bulk into an easy chair. There were dark stains of sweat under his armpits and he had lost much of his usual affability. He was edgy and irritated. 'You'll remember I told you that Fred Trainor, master of the *Sea Dawn*, had been killed in a car accident outside Paris.'

'Yes.'

'And that the man who was arrested for dangerous driving later *escaped*, and crossed the border into Switzerland.'

'I remember.'

'It seems,' Lansley growled, 'that my sources of information are not what they once were. You get away from England . . . The fact is, just as I didn't hear Ruiz had died in Guadalest, so I also didn't hear that Nicholas Bailey had crossed back from the Swiss mountains into Spain.'

'You mean it was this man Bailey who was in the car behind me?'

'The same.'

'But why should he come down here to the sierra to kill me? And who would want me dead?'

Lansley shifted uneasily and the cane chair screeched its protest at the movement. 'I've been stupid . . . I thought I could just stir things up a bit, get what I wanted . . . But I hadn't thought . . .'

'Lansley, you'd better start telling me what the hell's been going on,' Eric said coldly.

Lansley clattered his glass down on the table at his elbow. He was a man who had always enjoyed controlling situations: even when he had finally been arrested and imprisoned in England he had still, in a sense, remained in control, having bargaining positions to offer the authorities to secure an early release, retirement to the south of France and Spain, and continuation of his discreetly nefarious activities. But events had seemingly got out of control, rattled him, and he was angry, the fat cat who had seen the mouse he had been playing with slip away from under his claws. 'All right, Ward, I owe you an explanation. The fact is I've been less than honest with you.'

'I believe it!'

Lansley sighed. 'You asked me about the owners of the *Sea Dawn*.'

'Brandon Roskill.'

'Right. I told you they'd gone into liquidation. I suggested there was little information available to you about them.'

'I managed to get precisely nothing,' Eric admitted. 'Yes, but I hadn't been open with you.'

'So?'

Lansley stirred uneasily, glaring moodily at his drink, unwilling even at this stage to disclose anything he did not need to. 'The fact is Brandon Roskill never was intended to outlast the *Sea Dawn* operation. It's been a flourishing business in the past, but it was little more than a shell company two years ago when it was taken over by a group of . . . entrepreneurs—'

'Who are?'

'Let's just say they consist of a group of European businessmen who have, from time to time, worked together with a view to profit.'

'And you—'

Lansley wrinkled his nose in irritation. 'Yes, all right, I was one of them. I was a director of Brandon Roskill before the company went into liquidation.'

Eric stared at the fat man silently for a while. Lansley was still looking into his glass as though he might there find answers to puzzles that so far eluded him. Or it might have been an act, this image of regret: Eric didn't trust Lansley, from past experience, and he was treading warily now. 'You'd better tell me the whole story.'

'The *whole* story?' Something of Lansley's Pickwickian enjoyment of life returned to his pudgy, mottled features for a moment. 'Hardly that, dear boy. It would take too long, delve too deeply, for sure. Not the whole story, but enough of it to put you in the picture. And maybe to get you on my side, openly.'

'Why would I do that?

'Because we've always been on the same side, in a sense. All right, maybe I have to admit you weren't to know that, or that I wanted to use you to get my own ends, but believe me we do have interests in common. I'd hoped to keep my part in it . . . *submerged*, with the *Sea Dawn*.' Lansley grinned, pleased with the comment. 'Now, all right, I'll have to come out in the open because the going's getting too rough.'

Anger prickled in Eric's veins as he stared at the fat man in the cane chair. 'I've been down this track before, Lansley. You enjoy playing with people's lives, don't you?'

'A fault I freely admit to, my boy. I'm not alone in that predilection, of course. But what makes me unhappy is when people start playing cards they shouldn't, in a game I helped set up and should be controlling. Very unhappy.'

'Any game you set up is bound to be crooked.'

Lansley held up a fat, querulous hand. 'Define your terms, Ward. I have information from England which tells me you've been playing some funny games yourself just recently . . . In most large business transactions there are . . . *grey* areas where one is perhaps not treading a completely legitimate line. But if all parties to the transaction know it, where's the harm? If we all know the risks, why should there be a squeal when someone gets hurt?'

'Someone innocent?'

'Ah. There you are. But just who do you count among the innocent? But that's by the way. The fact is any game I set up may well have elements of . . . illegality, as you suggest. But there are still rules that have to be adhered to. And

I don't like cheats who take a hand, and then *extend* the rules by engaging a joker to help them win the hand.'

'A joker?'

'A professional killer. Like an Englishman, called Nicholas Bailey.'

CHAPTER 5

Reuben Podmore was sweating.

His office was airless and the window was closed, as though he feared the entry of more bad news. There was a worried expression in his sad eyes and his hangdog appearance made him seem heavier in the face, his jowls sagging despondently, weighted down with worry. Eric waited, while Podmore's secretary brought them a cup of coffee each, and said nothing. Podmore was too worried to separate his fingers: he had them laced together tightly, as though he was clinging to the vestiges of hope.

'Mr Channing's taking the matter to the board,' he blurted out at last.

'He can't dismiss you,' Eric soothed. 'It was my decision, not yours. You have a clear conscience. You advised against the action, and then did as any investment manager would be forced to do: carry out my instructions.'

'Mr Channing doesn't see it that way.'

'You must leave Mr Channing to me,' Eric said, but was aware that the confidence he had injected into his tone was not reaching the investment manager of Stanley Investments. 'Anyway, just how bad is the situation?'

'Worse than I'd predicted. The market has been extremely volatile of late, as you know — as I *warned* you! The international situation merely exacerbated a position that was already bad. There was an immediate reaction when the shares dipped, and the market went quiet, but then there was the scramble I feared, and it looks as though we'll be stuck with the issue for months, with large interest to pay, and at the end of it we might have to unload them at a loss. It's a bad business, Mr Ward. This just about sums it up.'

He handed Eric a newspaper cutting as his secretary came in with the coffee. Eric read the article, snipped from the financial press at the weekend, as he sipped his coffee.

* * *

A case in point is the Deutsche Bank Eurobond issue which caused such a stir when it hit the market. It seems a dozen firms and more were telephoning and telexing Bonn as soon as the issue was announced, begging to be allowed to do it more cheaply than the rate predicted. The bank settled for a tombstone of accredited dealers but, inevitably, ranks were broken and a few sharks lazed their way into the pool. Firms that were unable to get mandates started to wring their hands, cursing the supposed insanity of the sharks, who'd won business by offering to issue the Eurobonds with an interest rate shaved way below the realistic figure.

But then, the reversal! Suddenly the lunches held by the losers looked like being jollier affairs — and still do. They could look at the state of the market and with a combination of hindsight and sour grapes agree they were well out of it, and never really wanted to be in anyway. Banks that got scarred in the rush to the issue have been speaking of bitter days and of their confidence now that rates will continue to move upwards — leaving the main issue a successful one. As for the sharks, they should never have started prowling in such waters, because with the interest rates moving up, instead of down, their low interest bonds become even less attractive on the marketplace. So the signs are they'll be stuck with them, and the big names on the tombstones can breathe a sigh of relief.

For this time the crazy relationship between prestige and profit has worked. There are times when the demand for bank visibility and market share can run ahead of a concern about profitability. This time, it's the sharks who are getting bloodied, and those guys who are aboard the schooner can't be heard setting up a wail of regret . . .

* * *

'Interesting,' Eric commented, and handed the cutting back to Podmore.

'So what do we do now?' Podmore asked unhappily.

It was something Eric had already discussed with Anne. His return to Sedleigh Hall had not been an easy one. He felt unable to tell her the details of his trip to Spain, particularly the events on the road above Parcent, and the fact that she had been talking to Mark Fenham about the Eurobond issue left a certain barrier of resentment between them that would take a little time to break down.

It was an unspecific resentment in its terms. It might have been better if Eric could have discussed it openly with her but she was clearly nervous about doing so: she felt a certain guilt about the fact she had consulted Fenham at all, not least when she knew a certain edge had crept between the two men as a result of Fenham's close relationship with Leonard Channing. Equally, though neither knew for sure that Fenham had warned Channing about the entry of Stanley Investments into the Eurobond issue — it was possible he could have picked it up on the financial grapevine — it was another reason for reticence in discussing the matter. Neither wanted an open battle about the rights and wrongs of the business: whether Eric had been right in not keeping her fully informed; and whether Anne had been right in turning for advice to a man her husband no longer trusted.

Nor could Eric explain to her what he intended to do about the *Sea Dawn* affair. She heard his cool conversation with Leonard Channing, a conversation which was punctuated with long silences from Eric while Channing indulged in long bouts of vituperation at the other end of the phone. She was aware that Eric had insisted upon a meeting with the Storcaster Syndicate representatives at Channing's office as early as possible, but she did not know what was to transpire there. It was perhaps better she did not know, for Eric was still guessing, and relying upon a story told to him by the fat man in Javea, a man he had every reason not to trust.

His homecoming was therefore somewhat muted. There was a brittleness about their conversation, a forced brightness on her part, a certain preoccupation on his. They made love, but Eric was left with the feeling that they had both done it for the other and for the sake of the relationship, with neither deriving much pleasure, merely attempting to give.

Perhaps that wasn't a bad thing in itself, but it was less than honest.

He walked in the woods and across the fell at the weekend, and spent two days in London with Olsen, the marine investigator. There were ends to be tied up, facts confirmed before he faced the Storcaster Syndicate representatives. And he pored over the reports of the hearings before the court and before the Commissioner of Wrecks.

The crisp phone call from Leonard Channing finally set it all up.

'The meeting is arranged for eleven o'clock at my office, Ward. I would appreciate your arriving at ten thirty, in order that I may apprise you of the steps I shall be taking in relation to your vicious conduct over the matter of the Eurobond issues.'

Eric promised he would be there.

Now, when he told Podmore, the investment manager hardly seemed pleased at the prospect for Eric, nor the picture of the future that he envisaged.

* * *

Eric disliked travelling overnight by train so he took the afternoon express to London and booked in at his club. He dined in the club that evening and then went to the library, where he took the opportunity to relax with his papers, going over them a final time and reflecting upon what he was going to say the next morning and the tactics he might best employ.

He was still worried, of course; the prickle behind his eyes emphasized the nervous tension he was still subject to, because he was relying upon facts presented to him by Lansley. He had checked out what he could with Olsen and much of what Lansley had told him would seem to have a basis in fact, but that was another thing from saying that Lansley was telling the truth. Moreover, although he could understand the motives behind Lansley's actions, they were nevertheless sufficiently vague to cause him doubt.

He trusted that the next morning would resolve those doubts.

* * *

He did not sleep well and was somewhat late for breakfast, but still in plenty of time for the taxi he'd arranged to take him across town to Lombard Street. Unfortunately, when the driver took a side street to shorten the distance he found himself trapped behind an accident, involving a lorry carrying vegetables that had spilled across the road, and a Rolls Royce, the owner of which was in a mighty rage. He and the lorry-driver were engaged in an altercation that was noisy and lengthy: Eric's guess was that it would continue until police arrived and that in itself would be difficult since the road was practically closed by the traffic that had built up behind Eric's taxi. After a fifteen-minute wait Eric decided to cut his losses: he paid off the taxi-driver, left the cab and made the journey to the offices of Martin and Channing on foot.

It meant, inevitably, that he was late. The meeting with the Storcaster people was scheduled for eleven: there was no prospect now that Eric could have his meeting with Leonard

Channing before that confrontation. He walked quickly through the doors of the drab building and took the lift up to Leonard Channing's floor. The arrogant female secretary made no attempt to hide either her annoyance or relief when he entered: she buzzed Channing's office immediately and then ushered him into the presence.

Leonard Channing was standing near his leather-topped desk with a sheaf of papers in his hand. He wore a light grey suit, unusual for a business conference, well-cut and elegant, but his face was tight, and his nostrils pinched. He looked as though he was holding himself on a tight rein, anger seething below the surface of his polished manner. His voice was cold and controlled, nevertheless. 'You've finally made it then, Ward.'

'I'm sorry, I was delayed by a street accident,' Eric explained. His glance slipped past Channing, to note with faint surprise that Mark Fenham was standing near the window, self-effacingly. He had not realized that Channing and Fenham had come that much closer in their relationship: the young lawyer working for his wife clearly still hoped to be offered something by the chairman of Martin and Channing.

'There's hardly time now for our own meeting,' Channing announced snappishly. 'The Storcaster people have already arrived.'

'I imagine we'll have the opportunity for a discussion after we've concluded business over the *Sea Dawn*,' Eric suggested mildly.

Channing's eyebrows lifted ironically. 'So you've come prepared to conclude the *Sea Dawn* fiasco, have you? That's something, at least. As for our *discussion*, as you call it, I'm afraid you've been left with the wrong impression somehow. I can't see the need for much discussion. The facts of the matter are that with short term interest rates in New York not falling, with the European money market already glutted and several billion dollars' worth of bonds sculling around on offer, all syndicates are left with issues on their hands. Oh, I've no doubt we'll sell them eventually, but "eventually" can be a long time in moving markets, with the prospect of underwriters having bonds on their books for months, and eventually selling at below the price we paid. And even if Martin and Channing do manage to move the issue any profit made is likely to be wiped out by the losses arising from the raid you made — under our own contact name — against margins we had already decided upon as a matter of policy.'

'Martin and Channing policy, not Stanley Investments.'

'It's the same damned thing.'

'You know it isn't.'

'I know it damn well will be after today! After you're hung out to dry.'

The buzzer sounded on his desk. Channing glared at Eric for a few moments longer and then flicked the switch on the intercom. 'Yes?'

'The Storcaster representatives are waiting in the boardroom, Mr Channing.'

'We're coming in,' he grunted sourly, and flicked the switch. His glance, when he fixed it on Eric, was filled with cold malice. 'So the hanging can wait until after this meeting with Storcaster. But don't imagine, Ward, I'm doing other than savouring the approaching moment!'

* * *

There were four of them waiting, already seated at the gleaming boardroom table, when Eric entered behind Leonard Channing. Saul Berckman, dark-haired, his swarthy features set sombrely, sat near the head of the table with the foxy-faced Alain Germaine beside him. Phil Daniels sat in a typically aggressive attitude, elbows on the table, head hunched between his broad shoulders, ready to play his usual part, the blunt instrument wielded by men of more subtle persuasion and designs.

The fourth man, surprisingly to Eric, was the Spanish agent for Storcaster, Cordóbes, the man Eric had found so unhelpful in Javea. A slightly built, wiry man with a sallow complexion and quick, nervous eyes, he seemed vaguely surprised himself to be here in the London office of Martin and Channing. His fingers were long and slender and he raised his right hand, stroking the thin pencil moustache he affected in a nervous gesture that recognized Eric's presence. Eric guessed he had been across to England to report to the others on his meeting with Eric at Javea: presumably, he had been asked to stay on in case anything arose from that meeting in their conversations today.

Alternatively, there was a more sinister reason why he had been asked to present himself at this meeting, connected with an incident in the Sierra de Serreta. His eyes flickered uneasily now as Eric stared at him; Leonard Channing marched to the head of the table and took his seat, gesturing to Eric to sit on his left. He wasted no time in preliminaries or politeness.

'Gentlemen, I see no reason why we can't start immediately. We all know why we're here; we all know the background to the situation we find ourselves in. I make no secret of the fact that I have been in disagreement with my colleague Mr Ward; my advice had been to settle the outstanding business with Storcaster. The delays, gentlemen, have not been of my making and have not met with my approval. Mr Ward, in his capacity as representative of our subsidiary, Stanley Investments, saw fit to countermand my instructions and at our last meeting here insisted he be given opportunity to undertake certain investigations. He has, I understand, now completed them. Since so little time has passed, I imagine the investigations will not have been particularly fruitful. That is for him to say. I do understand, however, from the *brief* conversation I had with him before this meeting, that a decision will be reached today. In my view, not before time. Mr Ward?'

Stony-faced, Eric sat silent for a few moments. He had not expected support from Leonard Channing, but he had certainly not contemplated a stripping away of even the veneer of politeness in the proceedings. Channing had clearly distanced himself from Eric, leaving him completely exposed in the discussions. It was unlikely he would even undertake to exercise a chairman's normal balancing role. The atmosphere in the room was electric as the Storcaster men recognized the hostility that was now out in the open between Channing and Eric: Saul Berckman's eyes had narrowed, Phil Daniels had raised his head like a wolf scenting blood, and only Germaine seemed vaguely disturbed and uneasy, his Gallic sensibilities shaken by Channing's cold, deliberate animosity.

'I should begin,' Eric said quietly, 'by outlining our agreement on the occasion of our last meeting. You will recall that I was unwilling to make a settlement of the underwriting claim because I felt certain issues had not been pursued. You agreed I should be given the opportunity to pursue them, notably, the issue of whether the owners had in any way colluded in the admitted negligence of the shipmaster in so far as it related to the sinking of the *Sea Dawn*.'

'Put like a lawyer,' Phil Daniels sneered.

'My contention was that Storcaster — and the courts had looked for no evidence of such intention. Indeed, I also contended they had made no check on the seaworthiness of the *Sea Dawn*, made no check on transactions, voyages, histories pertaining to the vessel; in a nutshell, Storcaster was interested in a heavily loaded premium to the exclusion of carrying out proper commercial defence procedures.'

'We merely followed normal business practices,' Saul Berckman interrupted mildly. 'But this is ground we've been over before.'

'I also raised the matter of the death of the first mate of the *Sea Dawn*, Karl Mueller—'

Phil Daniels gave an audible groan. 'For God's sake, we're not going to have that dragged in again, are we? Channing, I don't know what kind of control you've got over this character but something needs to be done. He seems to want to use every cheap trick in the book to avoid settlement of his company's obligations.'

Leonard Channing's eyes glittered. He made no reply, but merely glared at Eric.

'I began my investigation,' Eric continued, 'by instructing Olsen's, the marine investigators, to carry out checks on the voyages of the *Sea Dawn* since she left the shipyards. 1 now have a complete history of the vessel. 1 then went to Spain, essentially to check on two matters: an inquiry into why the master, Fred Trainor, slipped ashore at Denia when the *Sea Dawn* developed engine trouble; and second, to find out what I could about the owners of the vessel.'

Cordóbes leaned forward, his slim hands on the table in front of him. 'I met Mr Ward in Javea. But there was little information I could give him. Our dealings, I explained, were with Gaetano and Damant, through whom we obtained the business. The owners, Brandon Roskill, we did not deal directly with them, and as they have since gone out of business, there was no way in which I could be of assistance to Senor Ward.'

His English was precise, and clipped. Eric looked at him thoughtfully for a few moments before he went on. 'Senor Cordóbes is quite right: he was unhelpful. But in fact I did — quite fortuitously — make contact with the owners. Or to be more precise, I was able to talk to one of the directors of Brandon Roskill.'

There was a short silence. The four representatives of Storcaster stared at Eric expectantly. Eventually Channing barked the question. 'Well, who was it?'

'His identity is irrelevant at this moment,' Eric replied smoothly. 'But his story was interesting. I think it bears relating, as far as he was able to put it together for me.'

'Forgive me,' Saul Berckman said, raising his hand. 'He — this mysterious Brandon Roskill director of yours — he did not have first-hand knowledge of events?'

'Some, not all. Much he guesses at.'

'Then surely, we can all *guess*,' Germaine said. 'What's the validity of guesswork as evidence?'

'More important,' Eric replied, ignoring the question, 'he was able to give me facts as to *intention*.'

'I don't know what that's supposed to mean,' Daniels said grumpily.

'It's quite simple,' Eric replied. 'The intention of the Brandon Roskill group had always been obvious and certain. It was to perpetrate a fraud.'

There was a stunned silence in the room. Leonard Channing sat upright, glaring at Eric, a twitch of nervous excitement appearing in his cheek. He was the first to speak. 'You can prove that?'

'Brandon Roskill consists of a group of European businessmen, as they call themselves, who operate on the shady side of the law. Some of them, apparently, have legitimate business interests in France and Spain; others, among whom I count my informant, have always lived by their wits and indulged in illegal practices.'

'A fine source of information,' Alain Germaine murmured.

'The fraud the group decided upon, in forming Brandon Roskill, was straightforward enough. It was a traditional piece of business — a hull fraud. The first task was to find a suitable vessel, and then they could proceed. The rust bucket was the *Sea Dawn*. Oh yes, gentlemen, believe me, the *Sea Dawn* classifies under that description. Now we have a fuller history and previous valuations from Olsen's, it's clear the vessel was near the end of her useful life. Now the usual method is to engage in a number of voyages carrying various kinds of cheap goods. Once credibility is established — in this case with Gaetano and Damant — the plans were laid. A specialist scuttler was to be recruited. They found him with no great difficulty. His name was Fred Trainor. He was taken on as the master of the *Sea Dawn*.'

'You didn't tell us who your informant is,' Alain Germaine said nervously.

Eric ignored the remark. 'Rust bucket frauds are not uncommon. The shipowner and the master conspire with the scuttler to send the insured vessel to the bottom. In this case,

Trainor was both master and scuttler so problems of secrecy were reduced. It's normal also, because rust buckets can be tricky to handle and questions can be asked, to send the vessel on its last voyage in ballast, or with a very low value cargo in bulk. Few questions are raised when the ship goes down, usually; the hull insurers pay up without too much of a squeal because of the problems of proving anything untoward. So Brandon Roskill calculated. They over-insured the hull by claiming an inflated valuation on the *Sea Dawn*. Out of greed, it seems, the valuation was never checked by Storcaster, who were merely interested in the heavy premium.'

Phil Daniels began to say something, but Saul Berckman raised a hand, checking him, and the Bostonian subsided. 'Go on, Mr Ward.'

'Late in the day, the plan changed somewhat. Like all groups of crooks, they got a bit greedy. They decided not to send the *Sea Dawn* in ballast as they'd intended; rather, they'd load expensive machinery on board, on which they'd get a high insurance recovery rate. They'd also got a bit nervous, in case the issue, of a vessel in ballast sinking, raised too many questions, as they have of late. A credible cargo, and shoulders would be shrugged. So they decided to load machinery on board, raise the hull *and* cargo insurance and scuttle the *Sea Dawn* somewhere in the Mediterranean.'

'The information we have is that there *was* no scuttling,' Phil Daniels protested. 'There was an explosion—'

'I'm coming to that. The insurance cover was taken out with underwriters and the voyage of the *Sea Dawn* began. It was always intended to be her last voyage. But things began to go wrong. First, there was engine trouble. It meant a hurried visit ashore by Fred Trainor.'

'I don't understand,' Leonard Channing said coldly. 'You mean the *Sea Dawn* hadn't reached the place appointed for scuttling?'

'No, it wasn't that. Where a shipowner intends to scuttle a ship carrying someone else's cargo, he may well make an extra crust or two by selling the cargo en route before the scuttling. He'll get the insurance for the ship *and* the proceeds of the sale of the cargo. As for the cargo owner, well, he doesn't lose too much since he'll recover on cargo insurance anyway. It's just the underwriters who stand to lose in the end.'

'So?'

'In the case of the *Sea Dawn*, Brandon Roskill owned both vessel and cargo. And they missed a trick.'

'How do you mean?'

'Well, if you own and insure both cargo and ship, why bother to load the cargo at all? Shipowners can arrange the issue of false bills of lading in respect of a non-existent cargo and the truth will vanish beneath the waves. The underwriters still lose. True, it involves more people — but provided they all get a slice to keep their mouths shut, things should go fine.'

'Are you saying this is what happened with the *Sea Dawn*?' Germaine asked quietly.

'Not quite. My informant tells me he was quite miffed that he hadn't really thought of the plan: it was a trick he'd have enjoyed pulling. He was more miffed when he realized *someone else had pulled the trick in his place*.'

Saul Berckman looked thoughtful. He stared at Eric, one eyebrow raised sardonically. 'The plot is thickening, Mr Ward.'

'That's right,' Eric said. 'But it accounts for the hurried arrival of Fred Trainor in Denia. You see, when the *Sea Dawn* developed engine trouble he was in a dilemma. He couldn't scuttle the vessel off Denia: it would be too obvious. He couldn't allow a tow into port, for fear the truth would be discovered. The fact was, Trainor knew the *Sea Dawn* carried a substitute cargo of scrap, weighty but almost valueless. The industrial machinery it was supposed to have had loaded had been spirited away in the Marseilles docks. Trainor knew it because he was involved in the plan, and now he needed advice on what he could do in the circumstances.' Eric paused, and added, 'I believe that's when he came to see Senor Cordóbes.'

The Spaniard flushed nervously and sat upright. 'It is true. He came to see me, Senor Trainor. He needed engine repairs. I was able to advise him.'

'And beyond that?' Eric asked quietly.

'I do not know. I was unable to help him.'

'Help him do what?'

Confused, the Spaniard shook his head. 'I do not know. I do not understand what you ask.'

Eric turned away. 'What Trainor wanted was advice. He got it. He returned to the *Sea Dawn*, and the engine repairs were carried out. But his luck was still out. The vessel struck something and was holed below the waterline. It's then, my informant thinks, that Trainor panicked. He'd already had one set of people working in the engine room. He didn't want another lot coming out to repair the hole. So he decided to use a crewman with a bolt gun. And that's when the supposition comes in.'

'You mean this isn't *all* supposition?' Berckman asked, smiling cynically.

'Trainor pumped out the engine room. He sent the crewman down with the Cox bolt gun. Maybe he didn't know the risk of explosion from the gas still contained in the engine room. Or maybe he *did* know, and sent the crewman down anyway, seeing it as a way out of his difficulties. No more problems; no surreptitious scrambling around in the dark to scuttle the *Sea Dawn*. Instead, an explosion, a fire, and down she goes — taking a chance, maybe, but Trainor was probably convinced by then that the *Sea Dawn* was fated never to reach the chosen scuttling point. And whatever his reasoning, that's what happened: the gun caused an explosion, a fire, and the *Sea Dawn* went down.'

There was a short silence, broken by Phil Daniels expelling a sigh. 'So that brings us to the point where we all came in. All right, Ward, so the *Sea Dawn* went down just as was proved in court. And that means you now have no reason not to settle your account with Storcaster.'

'I don't think you've understood what I've been saying. Trainor, as master, was guilty of negligence. It was a case of barratry. If that barratry can also be traced to the *owners*, the policy is void. My information—'

'Your information,' Alain Germaine interrupted cuttingly, 'comes from someone you've refused to identify. I would guess from that he would be unlikely to admit in a court of law that he was involved in this barratry. Moreover—'

'Moreover,' Daniels took over, 'if I get your story right, the owner *wasn't* involved in this so-called barratry. What Brandon Roskill were involved in was an intention to scuttle for fraudulent purposes. But what we got was barratry by Fred Trainor for reasons of his own — nothing to do with the owners!'

'So who, then, *was* it to do with?' Eric asked. 'What the hell does that mean?'

'If Brandon Roskill were not involved in the sinking of the *Sea Dawn*, even though they'd *intended* to scuttle her, who was?'

'According to your account, this character Trainor!'

'But to whom was he reporting? Trainor didn't dream up the cargo hijack himself. He couldn't have carried it through by himself. He was working with someone, an organization that made all the arrangements behind the scenes.'

'I fail to see what difference that makes, even if it's true,' Phil Daniels said snappishly. 'The policy is void if the *owners* are involved in the barratry; the policy is void if the *owners* are involved in fraud leading to the sinking of the vessel. But by your account, they *weren't* involved in the barratry, and the fraud — the scuttling — didn't happen anyway! And if someone else, outside these contractual arrangements, sent the *Sea Dawn* down, that has no effect upon the policy. It's still valid, and you'll have to pay up, grin and bear it.'

'Not in one other circumstance,' Eric demurred.

'And what the hell's that?' Daniels demanded aggressively.

'Where the underwriters are involved in the fraud.'

* * *

A shaft of sunlight picked out the veins on the back of the Spaniard's thin hands. Somewhere in the room a fat bluebottle droned and buzzed, exasperated. The back of Eric's shirt collar felt damp and there was a dull ache behind his eyes, tension building in the room as he felt the eyes of all five other men boring into him. Leonard Channing cleared his throat softly, as though preparing to say something, but thought better of it, subsiding in his chair. His eyes had been startled, his mouth agape momentarily; now he had recovered his poise, and his eyes had a frosted calculating look as they weighed up Eric Ward and what he had said.

Phil Daniels made a spluttering sound. 'Did I hear aright? If you're saying what I think you're saying—'

'One moment,' Saul Berckman interrupted. His dark eyes were clear and glinting, the line of his jaw rock-hard. 'Let's put nothing in Mr Ward's mouth. We can suggest that his last remark might lead us to suppose he's implying fraud on the part of the Storcaster Syndicate, since we are the only underwriting firm in dispute with Stanley Investments and the matter of the *Sea Dawn*, but let's not say it for him. I think, Mr Ward, you explain yourself, or withdraw the remark.'

It was a line Eric would have taken himself were the situation in reverse. They weren't talking of insults in this room, they were speaking of defamatory statements. Leonard Channing was silent, leaving Eric to put his own head in a noose. The challenge had been thrown down by Saul Berckman. Eric's mouth was dry: he had only the fat man in Javea to rely on.

Halliday Arthur Lansley.

'When criminals attempt a fraud, and it seems to come off, the likelihood is that they're happy,' Eric said. 'It's what would have happened with Brandon Roskill; it's what *did* happen to a large extent. The *Sea Dawn* went down, the claims went in, and as negotiated settlements were about to be concluded Brandon Roskill quietly went into liquidation. They were not concerned with underwriting claims in the financial world. They were happy. Generally.'

The room was silent, waiting, as Eric paused.

'One director of Brandon Roskill — my informant — was not entirely happy, however. He's an odd man in many ways. Quirky, a criminal and a hedonist, yes, all these things. But he also has a sense of theatre and he enjoys life, and using people. What he does not enjoy is *being* used. And he felt, in some indefinable way, that life, that incidents involving the *Sea Dawn*, and his own precious plans had been manipulated in some way.'

Eric could recall now, in his mind's eye, the picture Lansley had presented at the poolside, under the dark sky, a cigar glowing in his mouth as he strutted angrily up and down the length of the pool, explaining things to Eric.

'The fact is, Ward, I had that kind of prickly feeling that I'd been conned in some way. Nothing I could explain. It's just that things seemed so peculiar, so disjointed. I mean, we knew the *Sea Dawn* was a rust bucket, dammit, that's why we acquired her! And it wasn't a surprise to learn she was getting engine trouble off Denia. There was no way we wanted her listing in that area, of course, because the patrols could have got out, tugs from the harbour, they'd have towed her in like a shot. But I couldn't understand why Trainor should have got so agitated as to do the fool thing with the Cox bolt gun. Either he knew there was danger in that gas in the engine room, or he *should* have known. He was an experienced sailor. But if he did know, and sent that crewman down, knowing the guy could blow himself to Kingdom Come, what reason could he have? Why the hurry? Our calculations would have been: Okay, so there's engine trouble, so we don't manage to pull the fraud this time because the *Sea Dawn* gets taken in tow, so what? There's always another day, another voyage, another fraud. So why the hurry to send her down?'

He had stabbed at the air with the cigar, weaving glowing parabolas in the darkness.

'The question bugged me. We got what we wanted out of the hearings, the hull insurance came through, there was pay-out on the cargo and it was up to the underwriters to sort out their own problems. Brandon Roskill folded its tent and stole away. But not me. Not Halliday Arthur Lansley. More and more I got the feeling I'd been *had*, in some way or another. It's not a feeling I like. So I started putting out feelers, asking questions round about, making use of my networks. For a long time there was nothing . . .'

Eric dragged his thoughts back from Lansley beside his pool in Javea to the present, and the hostile faces in front of him. 'My informant, the Brandon Roskill director, began to make inquiries. Not the kind made commercially, but by using underground networks. And finally pieces of information began to filter through to him. They took him in the end to a tally clerk named Arturo Ruiz. From the tally clerk my informant learned that the manifesto and the bills of lading on the *Sea Dawn* had been forged. The Brandon Roskill cargo had been removed at Marseilles, ballast replaced it, and the real cargo had been sold elsewhere.'

'Like you said earlier,' Phil Daniels grunted, 'what're the odds? This *informant* of yours, this Brandon Roskill crook, what was he losing? He picked up his share of the cargo insurance anyway.'

'What did he lose? Pride,' Eric replied quietly. 'He didn't like the feeling that he'd been used — not he, a character used to manipulating other people. Ruiz wasn't able to tell him a great deal: he was only a small cog in a big organization. But once the questions were out, half-answers began to come in. He checked more closely on Trainor's record, and began to wonder what part the master of the *Sea Dawn* had played. My informant gave Ruiz some money, enough to allow him to retire quietly to his mountain home where he could be safely tucked away in case he was needed, and then the Brandon Roskill director went after Fred Trainor. He never reached him. Trainor was killed before he could be contacted. A convenient death — but my informant guessed it occurred because it had become apparent that questions *were* being asked, and Trainor had shown he could react badly to pressure.'

'This was not the way of it,' Cordóbes suddenly said.

His hands were nervous, his eyes wide and scared. 'My understanding is that Senor Trainor died in a car accident outside Paris.'

'He died in a car crash, yes,' Eric replied, 'but I'm pretty sure myself it was no accident — not after what happened to me in the Sierra de Serreta.'

'You're beginning to lose us, Ward,' Daniels warned.

'And you, Cordóbes,' Alain Germaine warned. 'Do not become anxious. All these suppositions, these *fictions* Mr Ward throws up to us, they are merely ghosts and echoes and phantasmagoria — not facts! Do not concern yourself, and do not worry. You are observing merely the floundering of a fish who finds the hook painful.'

But Cordóbes *was* worried. A line of perspiration beaded his upper lip below the moustache, and his eyes were quick and nervous. Germaine's scorn had not soothed him.

'It was at this point that my informant,' Eric continued, 'became even more dogged in his feelings. He had been conned, he was sure of it; someone else had muscled in on an operation he had run for Brandon Roskill, had made money out of it, and was now desperate enough to cover up — even to the extent of killing Fred Trainor. The Paris police arrested one Nicholas Bailey for dangerous driving, but the killer of Trainor then, unaccountably, managed to escape. My informant knew the escape was engineered by the people who had been involved in the hijack of the *Sea Dawn* cargo, and that it had been they who had paid for the services of Nicholas Bailey.'

'Who is this man Bailey?' Leonard Channing asked thoughtfully. .

'A professional killer,' Eric replied. 'He died, after trying to run me off the road in the Sierra de Serreta.'

'This is *preposterous*!' Alain Germaine exploded. 'What are you trying to tell us? You must be suffering from delusions — murder in Paris, an attempt on your life in Spain, the hijacking of a cargo from the *Sea Dawn* — what this has to do with our underwriting claim defeats my understanding.'

'Don't forget to include the murder of Karl Mueller,' Eric added quietly.

Germaine's mouth twisted angrily and he slammed his fist on the table in a sudden access of rage. Eric was surprised: he might have expected Daniels to behave so violently, but he had assumed the Frenchman was of a less volatile nature. 'All this nonsense,' Germaine almost shouted. 'It's some kind of delaying tactic! You can't seriously be suggesting that the death of this man Mueller in some obscure northern town—'

'Newcastle,' Eric murmured.

'—that this death is in any way connected to our contract!'

'I'm suggesting just that,' Eric replied firmly. 'We can't be sure of the facts—'

'*Hah*!'

'But my informant makes an educated guess and I agree with him. Karl Mueller was first mate aboard the *Sea Dawn*. It's highly likely he was in on die hijacking of the cargo. Even if he wasn't, he must have had suspicions raised by the events preceding the sinking. After the spate of inquiries he lay low in Europe, and our guess is he was keeping quiet because he was scared. And then he took ship to England — after getting the man who was supposed to have the berth out of the way. We can't be sure why he was so eager to come by ship to England. It might have been because he wanted to travel quietly to his assignation, avoiding flights and ticket purchases. Or it may have been because he was broke, and wanted to get money out of his knowledge of the events on the *Sea Dawn*, particularly since he would now have learned of the death of Fred Trainor. It was probably blackmail that was in his mind when he came to Newcastle. It led to his death, and the dumping of his body from the *Gloria* into the Tyne.'

'This is all supposition,' Phil Daniels drawled, but his eyes were hooded, belying the casualness of his tone. 'You still haven't tied any of this in as far as I'm concerned.'

'My informant didn't want to be involved personally: he has retiring habits,' Eric said grimly. 'But his northern sources of information are sound. He heard about Mueller's death and was convinced of the accuracy of his guesses. He heard I was involved, and was flying to Spain to trace the owners of the *Sea Dawn.* He was one of them, and intended keeping his head down. But he couldn't resist setting me on the trail he knew would lead to this meeting this morning. Unfortunately, things got out of hand. Ruiz was dead, and then someone made the mistake of setting the pet killer, Bailey, on my trail. It ended in Bailey's death, and my informant deciding he'd better tell me all he knew.'

'Do I detect the inference,' Saul Berckman asked quietly, 'that if this man — Bailey, you call him — had not been instructed to kill you, presumably to stop your further investigations, your . . . ah . . . informant would not have told you the whole story?'

'Something like that. The Brandon Roskill director had suspicions, but didn't want to get involved. My entrance meant he could manipulate me at a distance and learn the truth — whether he did anything about it thereafter is problematical. But the attempt on my life changed his mind: things were getting hairy. If it was *that* important, stopping me getting further information, the ripples could possibly head in his direction since he'd been raising the questions in Europe. So he told me all I've told you.'

'Putting *you* in the front line,' Daniels snickered. 'I'm warming to your friend. He sounds a careful man.'

'But what exactly is he afraid of?' Alain Germaine asked quietly.

'A business that's been built up over the years. One that's quietly been pulling frauds on fraudulent men. The *Sea Dawn* is the tip of an iceberg: it's one of many such deals. Not massive, up-front business in underworld terms, but big enough and important enough to want to cover its tracks by murder.'

'You still haven't said—'

'What it has to do with Storcaster? It's simple. All the information the Brandon Roskill director ferreted out pointed to one thing: information. The business has to be organized by someone who is able to have inside information regarding the insurance business. Not only what's being done by way of hull and cargo insurance, but what the likely rust bucket frauds are. A practised eye, picking out the likely Brandon Roskills and their rust buckets. And it's good, sound business too — because when their own operation is completed the victims aren't about to squeal. They've got what they wanted — insurance cover. Why should they worry about the fraud worked upon them by way of the hijacked cargo? Normally, they'd shrug their shoulders and turn their backs.'

'But not your friends from Brandon Roskill,' Germaine murmured.

'As I said, he likes to manipulate — not *be* manipulated.'

Phil Daniels sat up straight in his chair and folded his arms across his chest. His jaw jutted pugnaciously as he said, 'I been asking the question, but you keep giving me no answer. All right, so it's a great story, and maybe underwriting gives a guy the kind of background and inside information to pull the kind of tricks you been talking about. But you're saying Storcaster is the syndicate with dirty fingers?' He grinned, wolfishly. 'Because if you are, friend, you're going to have to prove it.'

'I can't,' Eric said blandly. 'Then what the hell—'

'What I can do is place facts at the disposal of the police, relating to the *Sea Dawn*. Then it's up to them.'

'The facts you've given us? They won't—'

'Those facts, together with two questions. The facts I've given you are a chain of circumstances. There are two missing links in that chain. I think we might find those links this morning.'

They were all silent for a few moments. The buzzing of the bluebottle became insistent in that silence and then stopped abruptly, trapped behind the curtains of the window. 'So what are your questions?' Saul Berckman asked at last.

'Karl Mueller came to England, to Newcastle, aboard the *Gloria*. He was due to meet someone; he met him, on board the vessel, clandestinely, and he died for trying to threaten and blackmail Were there any representatives of Storcaster in Newcastle that night?'

Phil Daniels frowned, and shrugged. 'I don't know. I wouldn't even know what date it was.'

'*I do* know,' Eric contended. 'There were two Storcaster men in the city that day: I met them, in the office of Stanley Investments.'

He remained staring at Phil Daniels, aware of an involuntary movement of bodies about him. Daniels glared at him, a vein beginning to beat in his forehead as the colour faded from around his mouth. 'Stanley Investments . . . I was up there one time, trying to screw your damned company into paying up. But I don't recall—'

'Our meeting was brief. You were leaving Podmore as I entered.'

'And my stay was brief. I took the afternoon train back to London.'

'So you weren't in the city that evening?'

'No,' Daniels snapped nervously. 'And I—'

'Then I just have one other question that needs answering,' Eric interrupted. 'It's to Senor Cordóbes.'

'To me?' The man was scared. A pale sheen of sweat lay on his face and he was unable to keep his hands still. He bitterly regretted attending this meeting, but there was no way he could escape it now. He waited, tense, as, Eric watched him. 'What . . . what is it you wish to know?

'Quite simple. It refers to the master of the *Sea Dawn*, Trainor. He came ashore, called on you while the vessel lay off Denia with engine trouble.'

'That is so. He asked my advice concerning repairs—'

'No. He came for another reason.'

'I do not understand—'

'He came for instructions.'

'This is not so. I was in no position to give Senor Trainor any instructions.' Cordóbes wet his dry lips with a flickering tongue. 'I swear—'

'No. Just tell me. You were the local agent for the Storcaster Syndicate. You weren't in business to advise on engine repairs. And Storcaster had no official involvement m the movements or control of the *Sea Dawn*. So why did he come to you, if not to get instructions?'

'But I swear, I was in no position—'

'To give instructions, I agree,' Eric interrupted. 'But you *were* able to put him in touch, through your office, with the man he wanted to contact. My question is simple, Senor Cordóbes. Who was it in the Storcaster Syndicate that Trainor wanted to contact?'

Cordóbes made a strangled sound in his throat, but said nothing. Even so, he was unable to control the despairing glance he sent down the room to the man seated on Leonard Channing's right.

'Bloody hell,' Phil Daniels said thickly. 'I left Newcastle that afternoon, but *you* stayed on! And there was that business of the wound to your cheek . . .'

Saul Berckman's dark head came up. His eyes were cold and dangerous and his tone calm as he said to Eric Ward, 'A long and involved story, but one full of suppositions, guesses, and supported only by the word of an undisclosed informant in Spain. Not exactly something you can use, either in legal proceedings, or as an excuse to refuse payment on an underwriting contract, which is why we're here, after all.'

'I don't think my informant from Brandon Roskill will ever be needed,' Eric said. 'I've already placed a file with the police. It raises enough questions. And now, with information from your colleagues Mr Daniels and Senor Cordóbes, the question is can you come up with a convincing story that shows you *didn't* conspire with others to hijack the *Sea Dawn* cargo, murder Trainor, attempt my killing, and yourself put Karl Mueller into the Tyne?'

* * *

Later that morning, in Leonard Channing's office, Eric felt a release from the tension that had affected him during the meeting with the Storcaster Syndicate. Mark Fenham was still there, with a glass of whisky in his hand. Leonard Channing poured one for himself thoughtfully, offering nothing to Eric. His features were pale when he turned, and there was a suppressed excitement — the effects of the turbulent Storcaster meeting — in his eyes. 'Do you think what you said will stick?' he demanded.

Eric sat down wearily. 'Saul Berckman's guilty as hell. There are enough leads for the police to trace the whole thing through. Berckman's part of a group who've been working these frauds for years. His response to Mueller's blackmail was foolish and violent — they'll tie that to him even if they never explode the whole fraud ring.'

'What does this mean as far as *Sea Dawn* is concerned?'

Eric shook his head. 'Too early to say. It doesn't look as though the Storcaster Syndicate is involved in the frauds Berckman merely used his position with them to set up the hijacks. But if they *are* involved, we could argue that their fraud invalidates the underwriting contract.'

'What's your guess?'

'In the end, we'll probably have to pay. We can't show a link between the owners — Brandon Roskill — and the sinking. Trainor didn't act on their instructions, but on Berckman's.'

'So you didn't entirely win after all,' Channing said maliciously.

'I didn't enter the contract in the first place,' Eric replied. Leonard Channing glanced in Mark Fenham's direction and turned to pace the length of the room. 'All right, now we've got *that* bit of business out of the way, let's get down to the rest of it. Mark?'

Fenham shrugged elegantly, his youthful face attempting a commiserative appearance but his inexperience failing to hide the evident satisfaction in his mouth. 'The market's still unstable, but the way interest rates have moved my calculation is that Stanley Investments will have made a considerable loss on the raid they made into the Eurobond issue.'

'And your summation of the legality of the raid?'

'I've already made my views known to Mrs Ward. At best, it was an unwise decision. Legally, it strays into a grey area. Ethically, it is certainly an action open to some question.'

'As a result of which,' Leonard Channing purred, 'I'm placing the whole matter before the board.'

'You'd be making a mistake if you did,' Eric said quietly. 'A mistake? Far from it, Ward. I'm going to take you apart. I'm going to show the board just how reckless you've been, how unethically you've behaved, what financial risks you've taken and what losses you're likely to occasion Stanley Investments. I shall, consequently, be recommending to them — and I've every reason to believe they'll go along with it — that you should be removed from the board of Stanley Investments, that the main board place its own nominee in as managing director, and the whole activity of Stanley Investments be once again brought closely under the control of the main board of Martin and Channing. Your foray into Lombard Street will have been brief, Ward; your venture into the world of merchant banking disastrous. But then, why should you worry? You still have your miserable Tyneside criminal practice to crawl back to, and what have you lost? It was your wife's money, after all—'

'I can guess whom you'll be recommending as the board's nominee.'

'Obviously, the man on the spot who has already shown loyalty to Martin and Channing. Mr Fenham.'

Eric smiled coolly. 'So it *was* you who blew the whistle to Channing, was it, Mark? Ah well . . .'

'I expect the board meeting will be convened within a few days and—'

'I've placed the issue, Channing.'

'—once it is convened you'll be sent the necessary notices . . .' Channing's voice tailed away. '*What* did you say?'

'I said I've placed the Eurobond issue.'

The ticking of the clock was suddenly very loud in the room. Channing and Fenham stared at him in open surprise, momentarily lost for words. It was Fenham who spoke first. 'That's *impossible*!'

'Why?'

'The interest rates . . . no one would be foolish enough to take them at those shaved interests . . . it wouldn't make sense, you'd be in competition with Martin and Channing, and the other tombstone agencies, offering a better deal. You *can't* have placed them, Ward. You're bluffing.'

'I've placed them,' Eric reiterated. 'And at the same rates at which I bought in. At worst, I've broken even, though I think that taking the rates into account, and recent movements in prices and commissions, Stanley Investments may even have made a small profit on the placement.'

Leonard Channing stood stock still, staring at Eric wolfishly, lips drawn back over his teeth in a grimace of surprise. Slowly his expression changed. A shadow touched his eyes, a glint of calculation, and his mouth hardened. He took a small sip of his whisky, his glance never leaving Eric's. 'You've placed the issue . . . but with which accepting house? Or would it be with someone else?'

'I'm not at liberty to say.'

'The placement is with someone who does not wish it to be made public?'

Eric smiled blandly. 'Publicity is the last thing desired.'

'I see . . .' Channing pondered on the matter, his eyes hooded as he stared at the glass in his hand. 'The deal is, nevertheless, quite firm?'

'As a rock.'

Channing nodded sagely, expecting the reply. He raised his head to look at Eric and there was something different about him, a coiled awareness, a readiness to react more swiftly to an opponent he had until now underrated. He was silent for almost a minute; behind him, Mark Fenham stirred uneasily and Channing's eyes flickered at the sound. It was as though he had forgotten Fenham was with them. He half turned, stared at the young lawyer, then waved his glass negligently. 'Mark . . . would you mind leaving us now?'

Mark Fenham's handsome features paled. Shaken, he hesitated, seemed to be about to say something and then, without looking at Eric, he left the room without speaking.

Leonard Channing tapped a thoughtful thumbnail against his front teeth. 'So you've placed the whole of the issue,' he repeated quietly.

* * *

A light breeze had arisen in the darkness and the cicadas had fallen quiet in the pine trees. Below the terrace the lights stringing along Arenal beach had faded but the lighthouse on Cabo San Antonio continued to pulse out its warning signal while at the far end of the bay, beyond Cabo la Nao, the horizon was lightening, the first touch of dawn fingering the sky. Halliday Arthur Lansley had not been pleased, slamming his glass down on the table, slightly drunk and belligerent. 'It's bloody *blackmail*!' he almost shouted. 'I thought you were my friend, Ward! The way I've just helped you—'

'You set me up,' Eric interrupted, 'and for the second time. Don't talk of helping me — you tried to *use* me and now it's blown up in your face. With the going getting rough, you're scared. You started asking questions and the result was things have got too dangerous. And you want to hide behind me.'

'Ward—!'

'You want this hijacking group out of the way, for revenge, to achieve a wild justice, but you're afraid to do it yourself. You want me to do it for you.'

'It's in your own interests, dammit. They tried to kill you today.'

'You want to use me to get your own way, but if I do it,' Eric insisted, 'you still don't want to be involved. You won't testify—'

'I'm an old man—'

'You don't want your name dragged in—'

'An English court appearance could kill me,' Lansley had wheedled. 'English courts affect my chest. The weather, those damp beds in those dreary hotels . . . you understand, surely?'

'*You* have to understand, Lansley! If I'm to keep your name out of this, it's got to be at a price I name.'

The fat man collapsed in a cane chair, wheezing anxiously. His piggy eyes pleaded with Eric. 'Friendship—'

'Counts for nothing . . . your kind of friendship, anyway.' Something touched Lansley's blubbery mouth, a twitch, hastily covered by a wheezing cough. 'Ah, you're a hard man, Eric.'

'You're harder . . . *when you've* got the whip hand.' Lansley coughed again, and raised a fat hand to wipe his trembling mouth. The cough was changing suddenly, turning into a rumbling wheezing sound that itself quickly became transmogrified into a deep belly chuckle. Eric stared at the fat man for a few moments in surprise, but the sound was infectious, his own mouth twitched and Lansley was suddenly laughing. The sound gained in volume and depth until the pool terrace echoed and the noise bounced back from the walls of the villa. The booming rose, converted into a shaky treble and then collapsed as a fit of asthmatic coughing took its place and the fat man wobbled helplessly in his chair. 'Hey, dammit, you're right, you're bloody right.'

Lansley rubbed his hand over his eyes, wiping away the tears of enjoyment. The reason for them escaped Eric, and he waited patiently. Lansley shook his head and sighed. 'Dammit, you're right. And you *do* have the whip hand. But then, what the hell — it does one's soul good to lose every so often. Not *too* often, mind you, but once in a while. It sharpens the appreciation, know what I mean, it's *legitimate*, and it's a way of salting away my ill-gotten gains, to the benefit of European business. That *can't* be bad.'

He squinted suddenly up at Eric, the laughter still in his eyes, but controlled now, with a hint of calculation behind it. 'You'll be selling me a pup, of course — but pups have a way of growing into big bouncing dogs. I've got contacts: I'll be able to unload the bloody issue here and there, a few pressure points, a few favours, the odd whisper here and roundabout . . . I bet you, Ward, I bet you I manage it.' He grinned, writhing his lips back wolfishly. 'I'll manage it. Damned if I won't! You've got a deal, son: I'll take the issue, and place it, and you keep me out of this nasty business.' He chuckled again, explosively. 'And when I do make a killing on the bond market, I'll send you a postcard.' His laughter rumbled out again uncontrollably. 'That's it — I'll send you a bloody postcard!'

* * *

Leonard Channing replenished his whisky glass. He hesitated, then looked at Eric quizzically. Eric nodded: it was an occasion to savour. 'I'll join you.'

Channing was silent while he poured a small measure of whisky and topped it with soda. He handed the glass to Eric and watched him while he sipped it. 'So you've placed the whole issue. It doesn't matter where. The whole issue . . .'

'That's right.'

Channing sniffed cagily. 'Makes no difference, of course, to my stance on the ethical issues. Your behaviour has been reprehensible.'

'But you would now find it a difficult matter to take to the board.'

Channing nodded slowly. 'Matters can't be left to rest, nevertheless.'

'So what do you intend to do?'

Channing was silent for a moment, calculating. 'I can't trust you, Ward. But I realize I've also underrated you. You're a novice in the world of merchant banking but you've shown me you possess a precious commodity. Luck.' His glance was sharp. 'If I come across a man I can't weigh up properly, whom I can't trust, and who is lucky, I know I face a dangerous combination. So, I shall be taking to Martin and Channing a different proposition from the one I intended.'

'Yes?'

'I shall be proposing that the main board places a nominee to replace you on the board of Stanley Investments.'

'And?'

'And in return I shall be recommending that you be offered a seat on the main board of Martin and Channing itself.'

'I'm flattered,' Eric said ironically.

'Don't be. It's for one reason only,' Channing said sharply.

'So you can keep an eye on me?'

'Precisely.' A brief, wintry smile touched Channing's lips and he raised his glass. 'It's something we might drink to our new relationship, and what might turn out to be a stormy future.'

THE END

OTHER BOOKS BY ROY LEWIS

ERIC WARD MYSTERIES

BOOK 1: THE SEDLEIGH HALL MURDER
BOOK 2: THE FARMING MURDER
BOOK 3: THE QUAYSIDE MURDER
BOOK 4: THE DIAMOND MURDER
BOOK 5: THE GEORDIE MURDER
BOOK 6: THE SHIPPING MURDER

INSPECTOR JOHN CROW

Book 1: A LOVER TOO MANY
Book 2: ERROR OF JUDGMENT
Book 3: THE WOODS MURDER
Book 4: MURDER FOR MONEY
Book 5: MURDER IN THE MINE
Book 6: A COTSWOLDS MURDER
Book 7: A FOX HUNTING MURDER
Book 8: A DARTMOOR MURDER

FREE KINDLE BOOKS

Please join our mailing list for free Kindle books and new releases, including crime thrillers, mysteries, romance and more, as well as news on the next book by Roy Lewis! www.joffebooks.com

Thank you for reading this book. If you enjoyed it please leave feedback on Amazon, and if there is anything we missed or you have a question about then please get in touch. The author and publishing team appreciate your feedback and time reading this book.

We're very grateful to eagle-eyed readers who take the time to contact us. Please send any errors you find to corrections@joffebooks.com

Follow us on Facebook www.facebook.com/joffebooks

Printed in Great Britain
by Amazon

11661300R00120